'It's been a long time, Lee.'

Trent moved his hand and with gentle fingers tilted her chin.

'Beautiful as ever,' he murmured huskily, then, rumpling her hair, 'except for the wig!'

The tension was defused. 'It's not a wig!' Lee squealed, as his fingers gripped and tugged, tilting her head back while laughter danced in his eyes. And then the laughter faded and she couldn't see the expression in his eyes because his face was too close to her, and for a brief dreamlike moment she closed her eyes and kissed him back.

Dear Reader

We have a good variety for you this month! Alice Grey gives us an insight into health visiting and the problems people can encounter. In MAJOR INCIDENT, Grace Read explores the hectic world of Casualty where Rory thinks he's too old for Fiona! We introduce new author Carol Wood, who brings veterinarian work back to the medical list—we think she's good and hope you do too. And Judith Worthy takes us to coastal Australia, where Lee and Trent have a lot to sort out after twelve years apart. Enjoy!

The Editor

Judith Worthy lives in an outer suburb of Melbourne, Australia, with her husband. When not writing she can usually be found birdwatching or gardening. She also likes to listen to music, and the radio, paints a little, likes to travel and is concerned about conservation and animal cruelty. As well as romantic fiction, she also writes books for children.

Recent titles by the same author:

STORM IN PARADISE
A HEART UNTAMED

MORE THAN MEMORIES

BY

JUDITH WORTHY

MILLS & BOON LIMITED
ETON HOUSE 18–24 PARADISE ROAD
RICHMOND SURREY TW9 1SR

First published in Great Britain 1993
by Mills & Boon Limited

This edition 1993

ISBN 0 263 78069 4

Set in 10 on 12 pt Linotron Times
03-9303-52960

Typeset in Great Britain by Centracet, Cambridge
Made and printed in Great Britain

CHAPTER ONE

LEE DENNISON was too busy to notice the sleek silver-grey Mercedes glide into town mid-morning. The January heat was keeping most other people close to their air-conditioners, and only an old man, sitting on a bench in the shade of the jacaranda trees whose purple blooms carpeted the ground around the War Memorial, heard the faint knocking in its engine and noticed the New South Wales number-plate. His gaze followed the car's progress as the driver coaxed it into the forecourt of Dennison's Garage and Service Station.

The oldtimer watched the tall lean figure get out of the car and stretch as though he'd been driving for a long while. He had a straight back and wide shoulders, and even from a distance his muscular physique was noticeable. His shock of dark hair, dark eyebrows, and the jut of an uncompromising jaw gave him an air of authority. When he turned so that his whole face was visible to the solitary onlooker on Jacaranda Parade, the old man recognised him.

'Well, well, Trent Allingham at last,' he murmured on a low whistle of surprise. 'And about time too, Dr Allingham. Come to sell off your inheritance, I suppose.' He snorted. 'You don't look as if you need it.'

Trent Allingham paused for a moment as, after the air-conditioned comfort of the car, the heat wrapped him round like an electric blanket on too high. He walked across the concourse to the service bay, where a truck was parked over the inspection pit, in front of it an old model Holden propped on jacks, and stopped in his tracks. A pair of long, tanned legs, feet bare, dusty and grease-streaked, protruded from under the radiator grille of the car.

Trent stared at them. They were unusually long and slender, hairless, and with ankles rather too shapely for a man, even a youth. He dragged his sunglasses down his nose and peered over the rims. Were motor mechanics wearing pink nail varnish these days? He raised an eyebrow. Admittedly this was not King's Cross, Sydney, where anything was believable, it was Shearwater Inlet, a sleepy backwater on the Victorian coast, but maybe the old fishing port was less stuffy than it used to be since the tourists had discovered its charms.

A couple of straining grunts came from under the car, the toes on both feet flexed and one leg arched at the knee as though to gain more leverage. Then there was a clatter as something metal hit the concrete. As Trent cleared his throat to announce himself, his ears popped to a low and husky curse from the same direction, and the mechanic began to slither out from under the Holden.

He found himself saying to a bare midriff above frayed blue denim shorts, 'Er—don't get up. Is the boss around?'

A runkled-up, grease-spattered, once-blue T-shirt, and finally a head topped by short red hair, emerged. Vivid green eyes journeyed slowly from Trent Allingham's polished shoes to the top of his dark head, before Lee scrambled up.

The sun was behind him and, dazzled by the strong light in her eyes, she didn't recognise him at once.

Trent said, 'I'd like a word with the boss—about my car.' He jerked a thumb towards the Mercedes.

Lee automatically sucked the finger she had caught in the wrench and examined the torn nail with a disgusted snort. 'Wouldn't it!' Then she said briskly, 'You're talking to the boss.'

Despite the grease smears on her face, the grease and dust on her clothes, there was no doubting her sex. Even if her voice hadn't confirmed her femininity, the T-shirt she was wearing was a snug fit and it was obvious she wasn't wearing a bra under it. Trent, mesmerised, wasn't sure he had heard her last remark correctly. 'I beg your pardon?'

'I'm the boss. What's your problem?' The peremptoriness of his demand had nettled her, and her throbbing finger made her short with him.

He moved slightly, and with the sun no longer in her eyes, Lee knew why his voice sounded vaguely familiar. For a moment she stared, unbelieving. Was the heat making her hallucinate? She blinked, but he was still there when she opened her eyes, rock-solid, as real as he'd been. . . She swallowed the memory like a bitter pill.

'Trent. . .' She breathed his name in a small dry voice, flicking her tongue over her lips and instantly tasting, under the dust and grease and saltiness of her own flesh, the warm moistness of his. . . To have that kind of recall after nearly twelve years. . .

He removed his sunglasses to see her better, and a crack of a smile flickered and was gone as familiar grey eyes raked her face and recognition dawned on him too.

'Lee! Lee Dennison. Under all that dirt I didn't recognise you! Your hair. . .it used to be blonde. . . and long. . .'

'I've been a redhead for years,' Lee said offhandedly.

She wiped the back of her uninjured hand across her forehead and cheek, smearing the dirt clownishly. 'It's a long time since the Inlet saw you, Trent. Everyone expected you'd come down for your father's funeral.'

The grey eyes were steady. 'I was overseas when he died and my return flight was held up in Singapore with engine trouble. Otherwise I would have been here.'

Lee knew she deserved the rebuff. Her own need to be defensive was no excuse for rudeness. He was looking at her intently, and his direct gaze put her so much on edge that she turned her attention to his car. 'What's the trouble?' she asked, casting a speculative eye over the Mercedes.

'There's a knocking in the engine and she's a bit sluggish on the choke. If I could just have a word with. . .'

'The mechanic? As soon as I've fixed the Holden, I'll take a look at her for you.'

'You?'

Lee enjoyed his incredulous expression and for some reason it woke the devil in her. It was a way to neutralise the effect he was having on her. With a casual flick of her hair, she said airily, 'Girls do lots of exciting things these days. I wasn't just looking for hairpins down there, you know.' She jerked a thumb at the Holden and didn't tell him that she was really a nurse and that fixing engines was more or less a hobby. She helped out in the garage at weekends, glad to do something totally different from nursing, although, as she sometimes thought whimsically, it was just another kind of nursing really! But it helped her unwind.

He still looked disbelieving, so she played him along. 'Perfectly natural, wouldn't you say, for the garage proprietor's daughter to follow in his footsteps?' There was an unintentional sting in her words which she didn't realise until she saw a muscle in his cheek twitch. He hadn't forgotten.

'So you gave up nursing,' he said slowly, his eyes seeking an explanation. When Lee didn't give one, he queried, 'If you're the boss. . .?'

She told him, 'Mum died two years ago and Dad had a stroke shortly afterwards.'

'I'm sorry. . .'

'He can't work now. He's confined to a wheelchair.' Lee gave him an impish smile. 'He's still the boss, really.'

'It must have been a terrible blow for him, losing your mother, and then a stroke. For you too.'

Lee shrugged. 'Dad's never been one to say "why me?" so he's pretty philosophical about it. He's not too bad considering. He's paralysed down his right side, can't walk, and his speech is impaired, but he manages well enough. He's improved about as far as can be hoped for.' She eyed him curiously. 'I heard you'd become a very successful gynaecologist and obstetrician.'

His eyes narrowed a little. 'Where did you hear that?'

'You know what small town gossip is like.' She couldn't resist adding, 'Naturally there's been some speculation about you lately, Trent. Ever since your father died, everyone's been wondering whether you'd turn up or not.' She added belatedly, 'You've lost both your parents. I'm sorry, Trent.' She wondered how much he really grieved. He had made a fleeting appearance at his mother's funeral seven or eight years ago, so she'd heard, but no one recalled seeing him on any other occasion. Trent's medical career had evidently allowed little time for anything else, even his ageing widowed father. There were those who speculated as to whether he was still the heir to Hilsborough.

Lee walked into the service bay, picked up a wad of cotton waste and started cleaning her hands.

Trent loomed in the doorway. 'Shouldn't you be wearing overalls? You ought to wear protective gear while you're messing about under cars.'

His concern was unexpected. Lee raked one hand through her hair and laughed. 'I usually do, but they're in the wash, and it's too hot for longs today anyway. I was only doing a little job to oblige a regular customer.' She didn't add that her skills were limited, that she wasn't a qualified motor mechanic, but she had picked up a lot from Len Parker, who had been with Dennison's for years. She'd learned a lot from her father, too, as a tomboy teenager with a passion for engines. He'd always wanted a son, so he hadn't discouraged her. She knew enough to be useful.

'You mean you run this place now—by yourself?' He sounded sceptical. 'The garage and the motel?'

'Not quite. There is other staff,' she told him stiffly, folding her arms across her chest. 'Len Parker still works for us.'

'What on earth possessed you to become a mechanic?'

'Same thing as possessed you to become a doctor, I suppose.' Just why she was having him on like this, she wasn't sure.

'But you wanted to be a nurse and have lots of kids!' he reminded her.

Lee couldn't keep up the deception. 'I am a nurse,' she confessed. 'I work weekdays at Shearwater Community Hospital. I'm just a spare-time mechanic.'

Trent shook with laughter. 'You little. . . You were having me on!'

She grinned at him apologetically. 'Sorry. It's a bit galling that it never seems to occur to men that women can be as good at the same things they are. I couldn't resist a tease. But you needn't worry, I really can fix your car. Two years back in Shearwater has been long enough for me to learn a lot. I always did like tinkering with engines.'

'You did indeed.' He folded his arms across his broad chest. 'Now tell me you're married with six kids. All your ambitions realised.'

'Not all,' she said, avoiding a direct collision with his eyes, because lies never came easily to her. 'You don't get everything you want in this life, do you?' The last thing she wanted to tell him about at this moment was Shannon. That she was, in fact, an unmarried mother.

'Unfortunately, no.' Trent was half inclined to believe she was still fooling him. Although it shouldn't be entirely surprising that Lee lived back here, and was a nurse at Shearwater Community Hospital—that was the last thing he had expected. And a motor mechanic as well. He looked around, half expecting Max or Len to appear and blow her story, but the forecourt was silent.

Lee said, 'You're on your way to Hilsborough now, I presume?'

'Yes, I rang Edna last night. She's expecting me for lunch, and I'm late already.' With sudden impatience, he cast his eyes around. 'Is there a car I can borrow? I could come back and collect mine later if you phone me when it's ready.'

Lee shook her head. 'I haven't got a car. That's my transport.' She waved a nonchalant hand towards the motorcycle standing in the shadows. On impulse she offered, 'You can borrow it if you like.'

His astonished look delighted her anew. 'You ride that thing?' He walked over to it. It was a powerful machine.

She lifted her chin. 'Of course.' A short pause, then she added, 'You taught me.'

Trent rolled up his shirt sleeves and wheeled the motorcycle into the open. One long leg swung over the saddle and his large muscular frame hunched a little as he kicked the starter and familiarised himself with the controls. The motor was sweetly tuned and Lee felt proud of the smooth sound the engine made as he revved it, then eased it back to idling.

He patted the tank and said, 'Long time since I've ridden one of these.' He looked absurdly pleased, like a kid with a new toy, and in spite of the pain of memory Lee couldn't help smiling.

He'd owned a Harley-Davidson, she remembered, and as a youth had roared around the district with any number of different girls on the pillion, her included. He'd had quite a reputation. She pushed another more painful memory down.

He idled the engine for a moment or two longer, then revved it again and glanced across at her, smiling with a boyish enthusiasm. 'Thanks. See you later. We must get together and catch up on the news.'

'You'd better wear a helmet,' she said, and handed him hers. It looked ridiculous perched on his much larger head.

It was an odd feeling watching him ride off on her motorcycle. Lee shaded her eyes and watched him until he was out of sight. She stood listening to the sound of the engine dying away on the still, hot morning and decided not to try and analyse what the last fifteen minutes had done to her. Not yet. She would come to terms with it after she'd done the job.

To her delight, all that Trent's car needed was a simple fan-belt repair and a minor adjustment to the choke. As soon as she'd finished, she phoned Hilsborough. The number was engaged, so she went back to the house behind the garage and took a shower. After it she looked defiantly in the mirror. Red hair suited her better than blonde, she gritted silently, short hair better than long. She slipped into cool blue cotton trousers and a white cotton knit top. She wasn't going to be doing any more dirty work that day.

She made herself a sandwich for lunch and took it into the living-room, where her father sat in front of the television, his constant companion. Delayed by fixing Trent's car, she was late, so he had finished his meal, which had been delivered by the motel restaurant. He flipped the remote control switch to turn the TV off, and swivelled round in his wheelchair.

''Lo, Lee,' he said with slow deliberation. 'All OK?' He had developed a kind of verbal shorthand to make communication less of a burden, and minimise the stutter the stroke had left him with.

'Fine,' she said. 'A couple of customers for emergency repairs.' She couldn't bring herself to mention that one of them had been Trent.

'Seeing Michael this arvo, I 'spose?' he asked, frowning.

'Not today,' Lee answered briefly. Her father did not like Michael Farrow, a local pharmacist who had been paying her a lot of attention lately. But Max would automatically dislike anyone who might want to marry her. He had always been a doting and possessive father.

They chatted for a few minutes, and presently Lee phoned Hilsborough again. This time the phone rang and was answered in seconds, as though Trent had been waiting for the call.

'Your car's ready.' Lee was businesslike and impersonal.

'Thanks. I'll be right down.'

She was surprised to find that her hand shook a little as she replaced the receiver. And when she caught a glimpse of her reflection in the hall mirror she couldn't help noticing that her flushed cheeks made her high cheekbones stand out more prominently, and emphasised the green of her eyes. She was hanging about the garage waiting for Trent to arrive when the office phone rang. She answered it crisply. 'Dennison's.'

'Trent here.' His deep tones caught her by surprise, and she drew a sharp breath.

'Yes?'

'I can't come and collect the car.' His voice sounded odd, tense.

'Why? What's happened?'

'Calm down. The bike's OK, it's just that it's run out of gas.'

Lee was astonished. 'It can't have. I filled the tank this morning.' She paused, certain yet not certain. 'Are you sure?'

'Of course I'm sure—I'm not an idiot. I may not be able to fix a fan-belt, but I know when a machine has run out of gas.' There was a long pause before he asked in a cajoling tone, 'Would it be too much to ask you to drive my car here, and bring a can of petrol so you can ride your bike home?'

'Isn't there a spare can anywhere? The garage?'

'I've already looked,' he answered.

Lee didn't want to go to Hilsborough, but there was no one she could send. 'All right,' she agreed without enthusiasm. 'I'll be there shortly.'

Lee gave herself a few moments of pleasurable envy sitting behind the wheel of Trent's car, toying with its various luxury gadgets. There was a cassette already in the player, so she switched on, curious to know what kind of music he liked nowadays. Still a jazz lover, she noted, drumming her fingers on the steering-wheel as Duke Ellington filled the car. But, more powerful than the jazzman's music, Trent's own presence was all around her, evoking memories and sensations she could do without. For heaven's sake, she wasn't a teenager now!

Abruptly she stopped the cassette. She'd better get the trip to Hilsborough over before the past enmeshed her too painfully or Trent got impatient and started phoning up again.

Hilsborough, named for the transportation ship that had brought Trent's convict ancestor to the colony of New South Wales, sat prominently on high ground above the inlet, a grand old mansion with wide verandas dripping with iron lace. It even had a tower, and there were acres of garden. Beyond lay the grazing land that had been sold off bit by bit in recent years as Trent's father went into retirement.

Lee cruised slowly up the long curving road, enjoying the feel of the car's leashed power beneath her small strong hands, and taking in the view she had only once before seen from this angle. The road didn't go anywhere after Hilsborough, so unless you were visiting you didn't use it. Lee had not visited Hilsborough—except that once, because it was Trent's twenty-first birthday party and she was leaving to start her nursing training in Melbourne the next day. In a small town where parochial snobbery still reigned even now, the wealthy graziers' and the garage proprietors' families did not mix socially.

Lee crashed a lid on her thoughts and glanced out across the wide expanse of the inlet, its calm water glittering in the sun, dotted with yachts, the low hills edging its shores studded with holiday homes. Most of them had mushroomed during the past few years as Shearwater Inlet became a holiday haven for the frazzled rich and a retirement spot for the cream of superannuated executives.

With great care, Lee manoeuvred the car between the stone pillars of the entrance to Hilsborough. The car purred smoothly up the long drive to the house, and she noted with satisfaction that the engine now sounded like a well-oiled sewing-machine.

As she parked in front of the house, Trent ran down the steps. He wasn't wearing his shirt or shoes now, only a pair of brief white shorts. His broad bare torso, lightly sprinkled with dark hair, chest and shoulder muscles rippling under an evenly tanned skin, indicated that he was a man who liked to keep fit.

'Hello. Thanks for coming.' He halted a pace away and looked her over. 'Well, well. . .what a transformation. Without the grease and dust, the mechanic is feminine and—beautiful.' He gave the last word a husky sensuousness that wasn't all mockery as he added, 'You know, at first I thought you were a boy!'

He'd never been short on charm, and time had made it smoother than ever. 'Thanks,' she said drily, and forced herself to stop looking into eyes that were conveying far more than she wanted to see. There were fine lines spraying out from the corners now, a slight slackness in the lids, but the slate-grey depths were as compelling as ever.

Lee lifted the jerrycan of petrol out of the boot. 'Where's the bike, Trent?' She glanced around and saw it, parked in the shade of a jacaranda tree that overhung the driveway near one corner of the house.

Before she reached it they were hailed from the veranda. 'Trent! Tea!' Edna Powis, the housekeeper, waved and called, 'Hello, Lee. Coming in for a cuppa?'

Trent turned and said, 'Of course she is.' And taking the can of petrol from her hand, he set it down on the driveway, urging, 'Come on, you can spare half an hour. I won't eat you!'

Rather than appear ungracious, Lee complied. As they went inside, the phone rang. Trent motioned Lee to go into the living-room while he took the call. Edna brought the tea in before he returned, but, despite Lee's protest, would not stay.

Trent came back, pulling on a pale blue shirt which he didn't bother to button. He looked around and said, 'Dreary's the word, isn't it?'

Lee's gaze followed his around the room, which was cluttered with dull and dilapidated furniture. There were patches of peeling plaster on the ceiling and the paintwork was grubby. 'It's not cheery, no.'

'Dad let the place go in the last few years. I shall have to renovate from top to bottom.'

Lee raised an eycbrow. 'But if you're going to sell it. . .?' She had surmised that his visit was a flying one to make the arrangements.

'There's a possibility I might not,' he said tantalisingly.

'You mean you'd use it—as a holiday home?'

'Perhaps. . .' He paused, regarding her thoughtfully.

'It's a lovely old house,' Lee acknowledged. 'You could do a lot with it. It's a real family house.' She looked at him expectantly.

'For someone with a family to put in it,' said Trent.

'You're not married, then?' Lee eyed him over the rim of her cup. 'No, of course not. You're a free spirit, as you used to say,' she reminded him.

He didn't deny it. There was silence while they both drank tea and consumed fruit cake. Eventually, surprising her, he invited, 'If you've finished, I'll show you the rest of the house. You might have some ideas about what I should do with it.'

'Me? I don't know anything about interior decorating,' Lee protested.

He caught hold of her arm firmly. 'I'd still like to hear what you think.'

The tour started with the rest of the downstairs rooms, all of which were as neglected as the drawing-room, then continued to the upper floor. Since he wanted her to, Lee made suggestions about décor, urging him to restore its colonial style inside as well as outside. It *was* a lovely old house; her personal feelings about it were not relevant. 'I'm glad you're going to restore it,' she felt bound to say.

Trent stopped and looked at her. 'You hate it, don't you? Because it reminds you of what happened here?'

'No. . . Well, yes, I suppose I do. Silly of me.'

'I'm sorry. My mother couldn't help being like that. What else can I say?'

'Nothing. I wish you wouldn't say anything. Let's not talk about the past, Trent—it's best forgotten. Let's look at the rest of the rooms. I don't mind, not really.'

He looked hard at her for a moment, then abruptly resumed their tour. 'The bathrooms will have to be gutted,' he said, hurriedly pushing open a door to show her what he meant, eager now to end the tour, wishing he hadn't been so insensitive as to suggest it. He hadn't expected her still to be vulnerable. He could have kicked himself.

Lee pulled a face and agreed. Dreary was definitely the word for it. The house needed a complete facelift. There were only a couple more rooms to inspect. Trent walked ahead of her into what was evidently a guest bedroom, throwing his hands wide in disgust.

'The bedrooms are all like this,' he told her.

Lee wrinkled her nose at the mustiness that seemed to pervade the whole upper floor. 'Maybe you ought to consult the National Trust,' she suggested. 'The house is very old and might be eligible for heritage listing.'

He looked interested. 'I hadn't thought of that.'

Because his closeness made her nervous, Lee crossed quickly to the window and wiped away some of the accumulated grime. 'The view's fabulous from here.'

'Even better from here. . .'

He had moved so silently on bare feet that she wasn't aware of him behind her until his hands on her shoulders spun her round.

The room was quiet, so quiet that the buzzing of a fly trying to escape through the window sounded as loud as a helicopter. Lee tensed under his hand which moved slowly from her shoulder up her bare neck to her nape. His thumb rested close to the pulse in her neck and she could feel it beating as he no doubt could too. Beating faster than normal.

'It's been a long time, Lee,' he said softly, his fingers caressing her tingling skin.

'Time flies. . .'

Trent moved his hand and with gentle fingers tilted her chin.

'Beautiful as ever,' he murmured huskily, and then, rumpling her hair, 'Except for the wig!'

The tension was defused. 'It's *not* a wig!' she squealed, as his fingers gripped and tugged, tilting her head back while laughter danced in his eyes.

And then the laughter faded and she couldn't see what expression was in his eyes because his face was too close to hers. His lips came slowly to meet hers, and she let it happen. She let the warm softness of his mouth rest against hers, and she let him hold her in his arms while he kissed her. A warmth like the first tingling sensations of a perfumed bath enveloped her, and for a brief dreamlike moment she closed her eyes and kissed him back.

Then reality intruded and she pulled away. 'Flirtatious as ever, Trent!' she joked, trying to calm the rush of emotion inside. She headed for the door. 'I'd better be going. Dad'll wonder what's happened to me.'

She hurried quickly down the stairs and out of the house, Trent following. Without a word, he filled the motorbike's tank from the jerrycan, while she buckled on her helmet. She mounted the Yamaha nervously. Trent had thoroughly disturbed her composure and she was angry with him for it, and with herself for the weakness.

'Thanks for fixing the car,' he said. 'What about the bill?'

She flicked a dismissive hand. 'Forget it. It was nothing much.'

Instead of arguing, he said, 'Then I insist you have dinner with me one evening. You can fill me in on

Shearwater gossip. There must be a lot I need to catch up on.'

Lee was reluctant. 'I'm pretty busy.'

'You couldn't spare just *one* night?' he cajoled.

'It's difficult. . . Dad, you see. . . Look, I'll call you.' She revved the engine, signalling her desire to go.

He laid a large hand firmly on her shoulder. 'Take care on that thing,' he said, 'it's a powerful and dangerous animal.'

Lee gripped the handlebars. And so are you, Trent, she thought, as she opened the throttle and the bike surged forward smoothly. She lifted a hand in farewell without looking back, and coasted down the zigzag road back to town, firmly resolving that she would not be phoning Trent Allingham, certainly not be having dinner with him.

On Sunday Lee went to the farm as usual to see Shannon. She wouldn't be seeing her again for a couple of weeks as Callie was taking the children to Merimbula where her parents had a holiday home. As she did almost every day of her life, Lee thanked God for the Morrises. If it hadn't been for Callie she didn't know what she would have done all those years ago, barely eighteen and having a baby she wanted to keep, but not knowing how she would manage it.

Just as now she had not yet summoned the courage to tell Michael about Shannon, she had found it impossible to tell her parents she was pregnant, especially her father. He would have hit the roof, and more than likely would have tried to persuade her to have an abortion or give the baby up for adoption, but most of all he would have been so ashamed of her. She knew he doted on her, and she couldn't bear hurting him.

She'd met Callie, whose baby was due about the same time, at the antenatal clinic, and one day had blurted out her despair. The next time they met Callie, an ex-nurse herself, had come up with a solution.

'So what if I go home with "twins"?' she'd laughed. 'The more the merrier, and Nick agrees with me. You can't bring a baby up on your own and study to be a nurse. You've got to think of your future, Lee, and the baby's.'

Once her pregnancy became obvious, Lee had found excuses not to go home, and concealing it from them had been helped by her parents going overseas on holiday for several months. After Shannon was born, Lee had gone to live with the Morrises on their farm, which was nearly halfway between Melbourne and Shearwater, until, a few months later, she had been able to resume her nursing training.

Shannon greeted Lee with her usual loving embrace. 'Hi, Mum!'

Lee kissed her and then held her at arm's length, eyebrows raised. 'What's this? You've had your hair cut.'

'Marnie had hers cut,' Shannon explained, mentioning her best friend as she whirled round to show off the new short style. Lee knew a moment of regret for the long dark plaits. In her mini-skirt and sloppy joe top, Shannon was beginning to look like a young woman already. Lee felt a mixture of love and pride.

Callie said, 'Plaits are a bit of a nuisance. I hope you don't mind, Lee.'

'I like it,' Lee approved, and collected another bear-hug from Shannon. She linked arms with Lee, smiling up at her, chattering on as they went into the house, and Lee's heart quickened. Perhaps it was the new hairstyle, or maybe because she was more conscious of it than usual, but surely Shannon was growing to look more and more like Trent. She had his eyes, his dark hair, and his slow spreading smile.

CHAPTER TWO

'AFTER this weekend, I'm all for ZPG!' Zena Winters wiped a hand dramatically across her brow.

Lee glanced up from reading a report. 'What?'

'Zero population growth!'

Lee laughed. 'What happened?'

Zena grinned. 'Six boys, four girls and one set of twins. All mothers and babies doing well, I am glad to say, but you should see the staff! Wrung out. Worn to a frazzle. And poor Dr Collins has bags under his eyes you could pack for a world tour!'

'Poor man!' Lee said sympathetically, as she shuffled case-notes. 'But at least the mums and babies are all doing well.'

'Now they are,' said Zena darkly. 'You should have been here on Saturday night, Lee. It was worse than the January sales. Everybody rushing about and falling over each other. Then baby Griffith didn't want to be born and Mrs G was hysterical, and so was her husband. I thought he was going to punch Andrew on the nose once. As though it was his fault!'

Lee smiled. Zena tried to conceal it, but everyone knew she was rather enamoured of Dr Collins except, it seemed, Dr Collins himself, who was young, attractive and more interested in sport than females. He got his thrills, according to Zena, hang-gliding, surfing and parachute-jumping.

'Well, it shouldn't be long before the new wing opens,' Lee consoled. 'And when we get someone to take charge of the new gynae and obstets units, we'll be able to deal with mini population explosions without chaos.'

'What's the betting,' said Zena gloomily, 'the building workers will go on strike again?'

'Don't be so pessimistic,' said Lee. Zena always looked on the dark side, expected things to go wrong.

Zena went on, 'And who's going to want to move from the city to this neck of the woods?'

Tongue in cheek, Lee suggested, 'Some dashing young doctor keen to make his mark on the way to a city consultancy.'

'That's what I'm afraid of,' said Zena. 'They'll come and go like locums.' She frowned disgustedly. 'There's one candidate coming for interview today, I heard.'

'Good,' Lee said absently. She rose. 'I'd better get around to see the patients, Zena.' Zena was always inclined to stand and chat too long. 'I'll look in on our new mums first.'

It might have been a hectic weekend, but now calm prevailed in the maternity wards of Shearwater Community Hospital. Lee felt almost a pang of regret that she had missed the excitement. Not that she relished crises, which meant life and death sometimes, or wished emergencies on anyone, but anything that set the adrenalin flowing, tested one's skills and resilience, was a change from the humdrum.

It wasn't an emergency, but one of the new mothers was visibly distressed when Lee and Zena entered her room. She was rocking her baby, who was crying loudly, and tears were running down her cheeks. A junior nurse was standing helplessly by. She looked relieved to see the seniors.

Lee summed up the situation and smiled at the

mother. 'Are you having a problem feeding the baby?' she asked, and the woman nodded.

'I want to! I don't want to bring him up on a bottle. But I. . .I can't. . .'

Lee motioned to Zena, who took the baby and soothed it gently. To the mother she said, 'I don't expect it's all that much of a problem. Most mothers can breastfeed—it's just that sometimes it takes a little getting used to, for both mother and baby. Sometimes it takes a couple of weeks for a comfortable routine to be established, so you mustn't worry about it.'

'I feel so stupid,' said the mother, choking on her words. 'I thought it would all happen quite naturally. I had a natural birth and Darren—my husband—was there, but now. . .'

Zena said, 'The baby was a couple of weeks early.'

Lee nodded, glancing at the name-tag on the bed-head. 'And you were a bit uptight about it, I'm sure, Mrs Calder. Well, that could be a factor. All kinds of things can affect a new mum. It's your first, is it?'

Mrs Calder nodded, and a gleam of pride came into her eyes as she glanced at the now quiet baby in Zena's arms.

Lee said, 'We'll ask Dr Collins to come and see you. But I think all that's needed is a bit of patience. What's your baby's name?'

'Damien.'

'We'll give Damien a supplementary feed for a few days so you needn't worry about him getting enough,' Lee told her. 'You must take plenty of fluids to help stimulate lactation, and breast massage might help too. Next time you're feeding Damien, one of the senior nurses will supervise in case he's not doing it properly.

Babies aren't always experts from the word go, and he might need a little bit of training.'

She offered a few more words of encouragement, and when she and Zena left Mrs Calder was looking happier. The junior, Rose, went to get Mrs Calder some orange juice, while Zena carted baby Damien off to the nursery for his supplementary, and Lee continued her tour of the wards alone.

A short time later, walking back to her office along the corridor, one side of which was a window wall overlooking the gardens and car park, Lee paused and gazed out across the town towards the sea, and as she often did, wished she could have Shannon to live with her, but, even though it was more practicable now than it had ever been, there was Max. To tell her father about her daughter now might cause a fatal shock.

Besides, to take Shannon away from Callie's family now mightn't be the best thing to do anyway. She was happy and secure with the Morrises, who treated her like a daughter. Maybe when she was older, Lee often thought, they would have some real time together. Shannon was nearly eleven now. She sighed. There wasn't a lot of time left. Children grew up so quickly. . .

The sound of swing doors opening cut off her thoughts, and Lee glanced down the corridor at the two men who had just come through. She nearly gasped aloud as she saw that one of them was Trent Allingham. The other was the CEO, Bryce Summerlad. What on earth was Trent doing here?

The two men were talking earnestly and did not notice Lee until they were almost up to her.

'Lee—good morning!' Bryce's head came up with a cheery smile for her.

'Good morning,' Lee mumbled, her legs shaking. She

was aware of Trent's scrutiny, but she didn't dare look directly at him.

'Good morning, Lee,' said Trent, deadpan.

Bryce looked from one to the other. 'You know each other?'

'From way back,' Trent drawled. 'We both grew up in this town. And as a matter of fact we've already bumped into each other again, yesterday. I had trouble with my car and had to take it into Dennison's.'

Bryce was pleased. 'Well, I'm glad you know someone on the staff, Trent. It'll help you to feel welcomed back.'

A thread of apprehension tied Lee's stomach in a knot. She glanced enquiringly from Trent to Bryce.

Bryce explained. 'Trent is looking us over, Lee, with a view to taking the job as Senior Registrar in charge of the new gynae and obstetrics department. Personally, as I've already told him, I hope he says yes. As you've already got a home here, Trent, it should suit you very well,' he went on, while Lee paled at the prospect.

'You mean you've applied for the job?' she muttered. 'You didn't tell me.'

His mouth quirked and Lee knew he'd kept quiet on purpose, to pay her back for fooling him.

Bryce's beeper broke the silence that suddenly stretched between them. He said, 'Lee, my dear, perhaps you'd take charge of Trent while I see who wants me? You could show him around your wards and fill him in if he has any questions. Would you mind?' He smiled benignly. 'Persuade him to take the job, Lee. He's the man we need.'

Like a hole in the head, *I* do, thought Lee dismally.

As Bryce left them, she asked, 'What would you like to see first, wards, Theatre?'

'Everything,' said Trent. 'Can you spare the time?'

'Half an hour.'

She hurried him through both the maternity and gynaecological wards, took him along to the labour ward, the operating suite, and showed him the nursery and the day-rooms.

'Well, that's about it,' she said, as she closed the last door. 'Bryce will show you over the new building.'

'I can see you need it,' Trent remarked. 'You're working under very cramped conditions here.'

'We manage.' She smiled impersonally. 'Shall I take you back to the CEO's office, or can you find your own way?'

Trent glanced at a clock on the corridor wall. 'Any chance of a cup of coffee first?'

If he's going to take the job, you're not going to be able to run away from him, Lee thought. You're going to have to put up with having him around. Might as well start getting used to it.

'Come along to my office,' she invited, though not too enthusiastically.

She made two cups of coffee and slid some biscuits out of a packet, asking, 'How does this job advance your career? You're already a consultant, aren't you?' That, like many late starters, he had shown abnormal dedication and achieved rapid promotion, was about all Lee knew about him.

'One doesn't do everything for career advancement,' he said slowly. 'I just happened to see the advertisement in a newspaper, and I felt a sudden yearning to return to the scene of my youth.' He smiled. 'Foolish sentimentality, perhaps.'

'You won't stay,' Lee predicted.

He stirred a spoonful of sugar into his coffee thoughtfully. 'Who knows? I might get to like the place. I was born here, after all.'

'Prodigal son gives up lucrative career to serve boyhood community?' Lee knew she sounded arch, but couldn't help it.

His eyes had some of the storminess of the ocean in them, and inscrutable depths. He did not react to her remark.

'But Shearwater's so different from Sydney,' Lee insisted. 'You'll probably be bored out of your mind in a few weeks. Shearwater doesn't have much social life to offer. And it's full of tourists nowadays for the best part of the year.'

'Does it bore you to tears? You couldn't wait to get away, as I recall.'

She shrugged. 'I was younger then. I lived for years in Melbourne, but I don't miss it. It's a nice change to be out of the city. I like the atmosphere here—at the hospital especially. I'm beginning to think I'm really a small town person at heart after all.' She smiled wryly.

Before the silence that fell could lengthen too much, the phone rang. Bryce wanted to know if she had finished with Trent.

'Yes, I've finished with him,' she said, and caught Trent's eye. A long time ago, she added silently. But he'd never really been hers anyway. 'Bryce,' she announced, putting the receiver down. 'He's free to take you over the new block now. I'll show you how to get back to his office.'

She escorted Trent to the end of the corridor and pointed him in the direction of the CEO's office. 'I haven't done much to persuade you to take the job, have I? I hope Bryce won't blame me if you don't.'

He faced her with a direct gaze. 'I get the feeling you'd be happier if I didn't.'

Lee blushed, and hotly defended herself. 'I don't know what gave you that idea!'

He grasped her arm roughly. 'You don't want me here, do you, Lee?'

His touch locked her muscles and froze her mind. 'Don't be ridiculous!' she muttered, shaking her arm free. 'I don't care whether you take the job or not. It's all the same to me.'

His hand was still detaining her. 'Is it, Lee? Or do you feel uncomfortable because we were lovers once?'

'Once!' she said. 'Literally *once*, Trent. For heaven's sake, that was nearly twelve years ago. I can barely remember. And I'm sure you've had enough lovers since to have almost obliterated it too. If you come to work here, we'll be colleagues, nothing more. A past indiscretion is irrelevant.'

Trent looked at her with a strange conflict of emotions. Seeing her again had disturbed him more than it should have done. She looked different now with her unruly cap of fiery hair, and her bubbling youthfulness was overlaid by maturity; yet she was still the same Lee, and there was still pain and pride in her green eyes, along with that elusive wistfulness that made him want to hold her in his arms and take all her troubles for his own. And like a fool he'd rushed her when she'd come to Hilsborough on Saturday, instead of taking it slowly, getting to know her, seeing if she wanted to get to know him again. Her manner today suggested she didn't.

He said, 'Thanks for the tour.'

'You're welcome.'

Lee turned abruptly and marched back to her office, more churned up than she wanted to be.

'Lee. . .' Rose was running towards her. 'Lee, Dr Collins wants you urgently. It's Mrs Rigiolo she's haemorrhaging!'

'Hell!' Lee flew, everything but the patient crisis totally wiped from her mind.

It all came back later that day, however. After dinner, which as usual was sent over from the motel kitchen, Lee sat down to watch the television news with Max, but her mind kept drifting back to Trent Allingham, wondering whether he would take the job or not. She still wasn't sure how she felt about it. One half of her wished he had never reappeared in her life, the other unwillingly acknowledged that he still had the power to set her emotions in a whirl. Why did he have to be so damned attractive? But so is Michael, she reminded herself.

It had been an unsettling day and, although she was weary, Lee could not sleep. Trent Allingham's dark eyes haunted her, which was ridiculous. She hadn't seen the man for over a decade, not since that night. . .

'Oh, God, stop it!' she cried aloud, clasping her hands over her ears and biting the pillow hard as she buried her face in it.

The next morning Trent telephoned Lee at the hospital. She was not expecting it, and she caught her breath involuntarily as his deep tones announced, 'Trent Allingham here.'

'Good morning, Trent.' Lee was proud of her detachment, her businesslike tone that she was sure did not betray the sudden racing of her heart. She guessed he had rung to tell her his decision. There was a pause and she asked, 'Well—are you going to work here or not?'

'I've just told Bryce that I accept the job.'

Lee experienced an extraordinary conflict of feelings. 'I rather thought you would,' she said, although she hadn't been at all sure. 'I hope you won't regret it.'

She was convinced he wouldn't stay long. He'd be off back to the city just as soon as he'd set up the new department and seen that it was running smoothly. Trent wouldn't stay sentimental about Shearwater for long, of that she was certain. All she had to do was keep her cool for a little while, and then life would revert to normal again.

'You still don't sound all that pleased.'

'I'm sorry. I am pleased that we've got someone with your qualifications to set up the new department. That matters a lot to me.' Lee tried to inject some enthusiasm into her tone.

'Thanks. So how about helping me celebrate? I still owe you dinner for the car repairs.'

Lee realised she'd overdone it and stiffened in resistance. 'Oh, no, I don't think. . .that isn't necessary.'

'I haven't got the plague,' Trent said a little testily. 'Or is there a boyfriend who wouldn't approve? Actually, I wasn't thinking of a public celebration,' he told her. 'I was thinking of a private one. I found some rather good French champagne in the cellar. Edna would enjoy cooking for two tonight, I'm sure.'

Lee refused to be tempted. 'No, thank you all the same. I don't think I can, Trent. Sorry. . .'

'You've got a date?'

She hesitated a fraction too long.

'Lee,' Trent's voice chided, 'what's wrong with two

old friends having dinner together? Edna will be discreet. If you're worried about gossip, nobody need ever know.' A smile entered his voice. 'I don't go out of my way to invite jealous lovers to come prowling round thirsting for my blood.'

Lee could feel him laughing at her. 'I—I'd rather not.' The prospect of dining at Hilsborough, even without his parents being there, made her feel as nervous as she had all those years ago at his party. If only she hadn't gone. . .

He tried once more. 'I thought it would be an opportunity for me to update. You can tell me who's who in Shearwater, and give me the lowdown on hospital gossip.'

'I'm sure Bryce can do that,' she said stiffly.

'Lee,' he persisted, 'don't be so unreasonable. Have dinner with me tonight. I promise I won't make a pass at you.'

'Dad. . .' she began, looking for a last-ditch excuse.

'You're not tied to him every night, are you?'

'No. . .'

Trent took decisive action. 'I'll pick you up at seven—or is that too early?'

Suddenly Lee didn't know why she was resisting him. Dinner with Trent all at once seemed like a pleasurable prospect. 'You're very persistent,' she complained.

He was unperturbed. 'When it's to my advantage. There are a lot of things I didn't have time to ask you on Saturday.'

She shouldn't have let him win, Lee regretted, as she dressed to go out that evening. She should have been firm and not let his charm undermine her resolve. She'd given his ego a boost it didn't need. And yet she couldn't deny the tingling anticipation that ran through her as the clock ticked inexorably towards seven.

At five to she was ready and waiting. She gave herself a last critical appraisal in the mirror. The dark green sleeveless dress was simple but flattering, its colour emphasising her eyes and hair. She studied her face. There were dusky shadows under her eyes, and she looked tired. In fact, she felt tired—more than usual at the end of the day. A vague aching seemed to pervade her bones. Perhaps she ought to be going to bed rather than out to dinner.

The doorbell rang and she picked up her handbag. On her way out, she looked in to say goodnight to Max, who was as usual watching television. She had told him earlier that she was going to visit friends. Lee was relieved when he hadn't asked who, as she had not felt up to explaining why she was dining with Trent. He'd never had much time for the Allinghams. Snobs, he'd called them. If he'd known that she'd been riding around on Trent's motorbike for the best part of a year, he'd have gone up the wall. He'd always been very protective and would not have approved of Lee seeing Trent Allingham, so she'd kept it very secret.

Tonight Lee had, however, told Lana where she was going, as she always did when she was going to be away for any length of time, just in case she was needed. 'Don't tell Dad, please,' she had said.

Lana had merely raised an eyebrow and given her a quizzical smile. 'Or Michael? Don't worry, I won't say a word to anyone.'

'I'm only going because he wants to ask me about the hospital, and the local scene,' Lee had insisted defensively.

Trent was staring up at the stars, which, despite the

street lights, were brilliant in a clear sky. He turned as Lee clicked the door shut behind her and smiled dazzlingly.

'All set?'

'Yes.' But was she? Lee suddenly wished she hadn't let herself in for an evening alone with a man who could still cause her heart to turn somersaults.

At Hilsborough lights blazed from the french windows which opened on to the veranda, and Trent led Lee through them into the drawing-room. In the mellow glow of standard and table lamps, the room looked less dilapidated.

Trent waved her towards the array of chairs and sofas which were scattered around the huge room. 'What would you like to drink?' he asked.

'Dry sherry, please,' Lee murmured, feeling a bit like a pauper in a palace. Just the way she'd felt at Trent's twenty-first birthday party.

'Do sit down, Lee.' He was approaching her with a glass in each hand, her sherry and straight whisky for himself.

Nervously she picked the nearest chair and perched on the edge of it. Somehow the past and the present were mingled and she was both gauche schoolgirl and adult woman. Trent handed her the drink, a half-smile on his lips, and an indecipherable expression in his eyes.

Lee looked enchanting, he thought, but she was nervous. It disconcerted him the way her green-fire eyes flicked around the room every time they caught his, avoiding him. She was like a cat on hot bricks.

He looked incredibly handsome, Lee caught herself thinking. He was wearing navy trousers and a maroon shirt. He wasn't wearing a tie, and the undone top buttons of his shirt revealed a glimpse of brown muscular chest. His hair was brushed back, the dark waves hugging his head, and, unless it was a trick of the light, there was a pearling of grey at the temples that she hadn't noticed before. The way he was sitting angled to the lamp on the side-table, half his face was in shadow, which accentuated the smoothly sculpted planes of his brow and cheeks, the strong line of his jaw and deeply cleft chin. Steady on! Lee told herself. He isn't all *that* handsome.

'Edna and Jim have been at Hilsborough a long time,' she said into what had become a rather unnerving silence.

'Forever,' Trent agreed. 'Jim's actually past retirement age, but people like Jim Powis don't retire. And Edna would be horrified, I'm sure, if anyone mentioned the pension. Besides, as far as I'm concerned, they're family.' His voice lowered as he said with surprising emotion, 'Jim Powis was always a father figure to me.'

That startled Lee. 'You needed one?'

Trent stroked his whisky glass. 'You wouldn't have realised it, but my father and I were not close.' He paused, staring for a moment into his glass. 'We marched to a different drum, Lee. He didn't want me to be a doctor. That's why I started rather late. Without Jim and Edna's encouragement I might never have had the guts to do it.' He rose abruptly and reached for her glass. 'Another?'

'Just a small one.' Lee was curious about his relationship with his father. That there might have been dissension had never occurred to her. They had never talked about their parents, and Trent evidently didn't want to pursue the topic now.

'But I didn't invite you here to talk about that,' he said.

'You wanted to ask me about the local scene,' Lee agreed. 'What do you want to know?'

Trent had not prepared himself. 'Let me see. . .' he said, racking his brain for a question that would sound genuine. 'What happened to the MacReadys? I noticed the shop's gone and there's a supermarket there now.'

'Progress,' Lee told him. 'The Macs got an offer for the site they couldn't refuse and retired. Their daughter, Marie, had her third child only a few weeks ago. . .' Was he really interested in small town trivia? she wondered.

Apparently he was, because he listened with rapt attention as she told him everything he wanted to know about Shearwater Inlet and its inhabitants and gave him a run-down on hospital routine and the staff. He slid in questions about her and what she had been doing for the past few years, and Lee gave him the same careful answers she gave everyone.

Eventually Edna came to tell them that dinner was ready. As she stood up, Lee suddenly felt very strange and the room seemed to sway, and as she entered the dining-room she stumbled slightly.

With a look of concern, Trent caught hold of her to steady her. 'Are you all right?' he demanded.

She felt acutely embarrassed. 'I feel rather hot. . .' What an idiot he must think me, she thought, which made her feel even more flushed.

Trent's hands slid down until they were holding hers. He held them up to examine them. 'Such small delicate hands. I can't believe they have the strength to handle that great machine you ride or to fix the innards of motor cars. You have a nurse's hands, not a mechanic's!'

'Well, it's not all done by mirrors, I can assure you,'

laughed Lee, a little embarrassed. 'Size is no indication of strength,' she added, and applied some pressure on his palms to prove the point. The warm tingling sensation all through her which resulted made her regret the action. She had no intention of being susceptible to Trent Allingham's masculine charms.

Edna's approach made him release her and she hurriedly headed for the place set for her at the table. Trent gallantly pulled out her chair and pushed it in as she sat. For a few moments while he went to fetch an ice-bucket and the champagne, and Edna bustled out to bring another dish, Lee was alone. She wished she didn't feel so feverish.

Trent came back and looked anxiously at her. 'Are you sure you're all right? You look a bit flushed.'

'I'm fine,' she said, feeling terrible.

Trent opened the Moët et Chandon with a flourish and the cork gave a satisfactory pop. He filled their glasses, then lifted his to touch Lee's, saying, 'To you.'

Lee managed to say, 'To your new job.' She took only a small sip of champagne. 'Lovely. Such luxury!' Trent was looking at her in a way that made her drop her eyes to her plate. She felt better when she started eating. The food was delicious and the cool wine helped to dampen the heat she was feeling.

When they had finished Edna's superb avocado cheesecake dessert, Trent suggested, 'Let's have coffee outside, on the veranda. It will have cooled off now.'

Lee was thankful for the fresh air. Her head was beginning to ache, and her neck and shoulder muscles felt tight. She shouldn't have had so much to drink. Not that two small sherries and a couple of glasses of champagne amounted to a lot. It shouldn't have affected her. Perhaps she'd better ask Trent to take her home just as soon as she could do so without seeming rude.

Trent poured the coffee, then leaned back and looked out over the inlet where the water sparkled in the moonlight. Lee sipped her coffee, hoping it would make her feel better, but she felt worse by the minute. She would have to ask Trent to take her home. She had opened her mouth to make the request and apology when a telephone ringing inside the house prevented her.

Trent got up. 'I'd better answer that. Edna will have gone to bed.'

Lee staggered after him. She paused in the drawing-room to support herself on the back of an armchair. She felt most peculiar. She brushed the back of her hand across her forehead. What on earth was the matter with her?

Trent returned quickly. 'It's for you,' he said, sounding surprised, then, seeing her distress, 'What's the matter, Lee? Are you ill?'

'No—I don't know. I feel ghastly. . . Did you say it was for me? But who. . .?' Only Lana knew where she was. With Trent's hand guiding her, Lee went into the study and picked up the receiver. 'Lana?'

'Lee. . .oh, Lee. . .' Lana's voice cracked.

Lee tensed with foreboding. 'What's wrong?' Her head was throbbing now.

'It—it's Max. He managed to press his alarm button and I raced over, but—he was gone. Oh, Lee, it must have happened so quickly—a massive stroke. I tried to revive him, but it was too late. I called the ambulance—they're taking him to the hospital, but—you'd better come. . .'

Lee felt the blood drain from her face. 'You mean—Dad. . . Dad's dead?'

'Yes. . .'

'Oh, no!' White-faced, Lee looked up at Trent. 'It's Dad. . .' The receiver slid from her hand and she crumpled into a heap at his feet.

CHAPTER THREE

THE details of what happened after she collapsed that night would always remain hazy in Lee's mind. It wasn't until a few days after the funeral that she began to return to normal and the fog that had invaded her mind started to clear.

She was aware that for days she had been functioning like a marionette with Trent and other people pulling the strings. It had been like a nightmare from which she couldn't wake up.

Once she'd overheard Trent say, 'She'll be all right when the funeral's over. It's emotional and mental shock, together with a nasty dose of flu. It's hardly surprising she's temporarily lost her grip. Rest and protection from anxiety are all she needs.'

'I can't stay here any longer!' Lee suddenly exclaimed aloud. 'I can't. . .'

It was all flooding back now, details were slotting together into a pattern, and she was appalled at how one half of her could have known what was going on, while the other half simply refused to accept it or deal with it. Her brain had just tried to ignore everything, hoping it would go away. She was appalled at how ineffectual she had been, leaving everything to others to decide and arrange. That wasn't like her at all. She was usually so organised, so independent, so efficient. But she had gone to pieces completely. It was just that everything had come at once and she had snapped.

It was fortunate that it had happened while Callie

and the children were away, but they must be due back any day, Lee thought, struggling to remember dates. When she did, it was with relief that she still had a few days' grace.

That afternoon, she felt strong enough to go for a walk along the clifftops. The stiff breeze off the ocean buffeted her and tangled her hair. It helped to sweep the lingering fog away and clear her mind.

She encountered Trent as she came in. 'Been for a walk?' he asked, studying her face anxiously.

'Just along the cliff path.' She smoothed a hand over her windblown hair. Trent still made her feel nervous.

He looked intently at her. She looked different today, not so detached, and there was a hint of sparkle in the green eyes that gave him hope.

'You look better today, Lee,' he told her.

Lee was touched by his concern. He had been very kind. 'Very much better,' she said. 'I—I think I'm all right now. This morning I woke up feeling different.'

She looked beautiful, he thought, with her russet hair all tousled, her skin glowing, her lips parted because she was a little breathless. Suppressing a desire to kiss her made his voice croak as he said, 'You mustn't overdo it, though.'

She suddenly felt overwhelmed by obligation. 'You've been very kind letting me stay here, Trent. It's nearly a fortnight and I mustn't impose on you any longer. And I must get back to work.'

'You're not going anywhere until you're quite fit again,' Trent stated, 'and certainly not back to work. That flu you had was a virulent strain. You mustn't risk a relapse.'

Lee chafed at his orders. 'I'm fine now.' She knew

she wasn't, but she hated being ill. She insisted, 'I must go and sort things out at the garage.'

'There's no hurry.' Trent touched her arm. 'Don't worry, everything's under control. It's business as usual. Len Parker's taking care of the garage.'

Taking a step away from him, she raked both hands through her hair. 'I feel such a fool!'

'For getting the flu? Don't be silly. It's going through the hospital like wildfire. And besides, you've also had a shock.'

Lee didn't want to think about it. If only she'd been at home that night, she might have saved him. . .'You've started work at the hospital,' she said. She had been vaguely aware of it.

'Yes.'

'So soon?'

'I was able to organise things in Sydney to make it possible,' he told her, and with a shrug, 'Once you make up your mind to do something, the sooner you do it the better.'

She smiled faintly. 'Before you change your mind?' Their eyes met for a moment, and Lee looked quickly away, saying, 'How are you getting on?'

He pulled a wry face. 'I think the patients like me better than the staff do. New brooms aren't always popular.'

Lee found she could actually laugh. 'Oh, we have some diehards there. I daresay you'll run up against a fair bit of opposition.'

He smiled. 'I'm stretching my charm to the limit!'

Lee was still feeling her obligation keenly. 'I—I'm sorry for all the trouble I've caused you, Trent. I must have been totally dazed. Way off the planet, I'm afraid. It was strange I was aware of what was going on, the funeral and everything, but I couldn't seem to make myself *do* anything. . .' Puzzlement at the state she had been in lingered and she smiled shakily. 'I suppose I've had a sort of nervous breakdown.'

'It's not unusual for someone who's suffering from shock to shut off completely,' Trent reassured her. 'And you were ill with flu as well, don't forget.' He reached out and lifted a strand of hair off her face, tucking it behind her ear.

She jerked back, her awareness of him suddenly sharp. 'I'd better go and comb my hair.'

'It looks rather fetching all tousled,' he told her.

Lee started for the stairs. 'Just the same, I think I'd better tidy up.' She turned. 'I can't thank you enough for all you've done. I feel terrible letting you do all the organising—the funeral and everything. I'm very grateful, Trent.'

He strode up to her and grasped her arms. 'Lee, for goodness' sake stop thanking me! I only did what anyone else would have done in the circumstances.'

Her eyes filled with tears, although he had spoken gently. Trent couldn't bear it. 'Oh, God don't cry, Lee. I'm sorry.' He pulled her slender form into his arms and pressed her cheek against his chest. She seemed so fragile and vulnerable now, it was hard to remember that inside this softly feminine form was a spirited woman, proud, independent and fiercely honourable. A woman who could fix automobiles and ride a powerful motorbike as well as nurse the sick!

He held her for a long moment, then gently eased her away from him, cupping her face in his hands as he looked into her eyes. Lee swayed, mesmerised, and her lips parted in a protest that was never spoken. Trent covered her mouth with his, and his touch released a deep emotional response in her. He was not unaware of it and deepened the kiss slowly, while drawing her back hard against him. The kiss went on for a long time, and when they finally drew apart, breathless, Lee murmured, 'See you later,' and ran quickly up the stairs.

Trent watched her go, entranced by the sway of her neat bottom, the shapeliness of her slender legs in tight jeans, then, pounding his fist into his palm, he went off to cadge a cup of tea from Edna.

After dinner that evening, Trent ventured, 'Are you going to have coffee with me tonight?' He was pleased to see that she had changed for dinner and applied a little make-up, a sure sign she was getting better. In the slim-fitting tan skirt and tan and white-patterned blouse, one of the outfits Edna had brought over from the house for her, Lee looked fragile but lovely. He wanted to touch her, reverently, the way you would touch a piece of valuable and rare porcelain. But being impulsive was a trait he knew he must try to curb—especially with Lee.

Lee wanted to say she felt tired and would rather go straight to bed as she had been doing after dinner, but she heard herself agreeing as though some higher force had overruled her. After Edna had brought the coffee into the drawing-room, Trent looked down at Lee's small figure curled up on the couch. 'What about a nightcap? Brandy?'

'Just a small one.'

He fetched the drinks and sat at the other end of the couch. 'I know it's early days, but have you thought at all about what you're going to do with the business?' he asked.

'Keep it going, I suppose,' said Lee. To her it meant

that at last she had some real security, something to build on for Shannon. The reminder that her father's death had provided it brought tears to her eyes, and she brushed them quickly away.

Trent, watching her, said softly, 'You haven't cried properly yet, Lee.'

She looked at him, startled.

'You're bottling up your grief,' he went on. 'That's part of your problem. I could see that earlier. I said "don't cry", but really you need to let go, Lee.'

She shook her head. 'I'm all right. . .' But she knew she wasn't.

'You did everything you could for your father,' Trent told her. 'His death wasn't your fault.'

He had touched the raw nerve, deliberately, she knew. 'If I'd been there,' she said, her eyes misting over again, 'I might have saved him. . .' The tears now began to flow in earnest. 'At least I would have tried,' she sobbed.

Trent moved swiftly, taking her in his arms and comforting her. It was the gesture that broke down her defences and the floodgates opened. Lee wept on his shoulder as she should have wept days ago. At first her whole frame shook with uncontrollable sobs which, as she became exhausted by emotion, gradually subsided, and she clung to Trent like a child. It was the first time in years, she realised, that there had been someone to cling to, to snuggle up to when she needed them. Trent's fingers in her hair, his palm against her cheek, his strong arm holding her close, were balm to her soul, and it was a long while before she even wanted to move.

When she did, embarrassed at her outburst, and tried to apologise, he placed a finger on her lips, and cupping her tear-stained face in his large hands, brushed his lips across hers.

'Better now?' He was smiling as he wiped the dampness from her face with a handkerchief. He handed it to her and she blew her nose.

'I'm a fool. . .' she sniffed.

'You're a normal human being,' Trent said. 'Now you've released the tension, you'll be OK. I think a warm drink and maybe another small brandy to make you sleep.'

Wearily Lee leaned against the cushions. She felt drained. Trent came back with a tray and she gratefully accepted the mug of warm milk. He placed a small brandy on the lamp table near her, and sat down beside her again.

'Your father could have had a second stroke at any time,' he said. 'And you wouldn't have saved him, Lee—no one could have. There's absolutely no reason why you should blame yourself.'

'No, I suppose not.' She looked sadly at him. 'It was so sudden. I know I should have expected it, but you get used to a situation and you don't spend every minute wondering if someone is going to die.' She sighed deeply. 'Trent, it seems so awful not to say goodbye.'

Trent clasped her hand. 'I think you've said goodbye now.'

Lee glanced at him ruefully. 'I guess so. . .' She tried to remember the funeral. She'd insisted on going even though she felt so ill that day, and it was still a blur. Michael had been there, holding her hand, sympathetic, but she hadn't seen him since, had she?

The warm drink was doing its job and Lee suddenly

yawned involuntarily. She could hardly keep her eyes open. 'What did you put in this?' she asked.

'Nothing—you don't need a sleeping pill. I suggest you go off to bed right away. Tomorrow you can go back to the garage, but take it easy. I don't want you back at the hospital for another week at least, and you're only to do a couple of days for a start.'

Lee nodded. 'All right. I'll have a lot to do at home, I suppose. I guess nobody is indispensable.'

Trent grinned. 'We're managing—just!'

It seemed very strange to Lee living alone in the house behind the garage. Everywhere there were reminders of her father, and several times she imagined she saw him sitting in the wheelchair. In the end, she moved it out of sight, and day by day, almost unconsciously, she tidied away his things.

Trent called daily, and invited her to dinner at Hilsborough whenever she wished, but she always declined, and he didn't press her. He seemed to understand her need to be alone.

The time flew. She had a lot to do, dealing with accumulated mail, writing thank-you notes, answering phone calls enquiring after her health, and sorting out her father's papers, his clothes and other belongings, seeing the solicitor, the accountant, the bank.

Callie and the children came back from holiday and Lee went out to the farm. Callie, worried about her when she heard of her illness and her father's death, wanted Lee to stay for a while, but Lee wouldn't. 'Lana makes sure I eat properly,' she laughed.

Lee had one big regret, and that was that she had never told Shannon about Max, or him about her. Shannon thought the reason Lee had moved from

Melbourne to Shearwater was so that she could be nearer to the farm and her daughter. She had asked about her grandparents once, and Lee had reluctantly lied and told her they were dead. Now it was true. It raised in her mind the awful dilemma of whether she should tell Trent he had a daughter.

Michael came to see her and was a little resentful because Trent had not allowed her to have visitors. He took her out to dinner, and Lee tried to be good company, but her mind was elsewhere and conversation wasn't as easy as usual.

He was understanding. 'You've had a tough time lately, Lee. It'll take a while to get over your father's death, I expect. I want you to know that if there's anything I can do, if there's anything you need, I'm here.'

'You're very kind, Michael,' she said dully, and felt guilty because she wasn't more desperate for his kindness.

Taking Trent's advice, Lee went back to work on a Wednesday. As she parked her bike in the staff parking area, she noticed that a grey Mercedes was already there. Trent was evidently an early bird.

Lee's first stop after she had changed into her uniform was the CEO's office. Bryce was always early too. He greeted her with relief and concern.

'Are you sure you're all right, Lee? You look a bit pale. I hope you haven't come back too soon.'

She assured him she was fine and promised not to overdo things, though how that was possible for a nurse if circumstances demanded it, and patients needed you, she didn't know.

'As soon as possible, we must have a meeting,' said

Bryce. 'You, me and Trent. He has a few proposals for us to discuss.'

Lee smiled. 'That doesn't surprise me.'

'Including a grand opening,' Bryce told her. 'With all the media in attendance.'

Lee groaned, but smiled tolerantly. 'Well, I suppose it'll be big news locally, and the publicity won't do any harm.'

Leaving the CEO, she went straight to her office. Zena Winters had been acting charge nurse while she was off sick, and was there to greet her.

'Am I glad to see you,' Zena said with fervour. 'Another day and I'd have resigned!' She scrutinised her intently. 'Are you sure you're up to it, Lee? You look a bit fragile.' She added gently, 'I'm sorry about your father.'

'I'm fine,' Lee assured her, and for the rest of the morning she found herself endlessly repeating the phrase. It was gratifying, though, that so many people welcomed her back and were concerned about her.

What amused her was the variety of opinions about Trent she received. Young Rose Miller thought he was 'strict but gorgeous!' but one of the older nurses commented, 'He's rather young for the job; I hope he knows what he's doing.' Zena said he was 'a bit overbearing and humourless', but when Lee was asking about various patients who had been in her care and had now gone home, she revealed a healthy respect for his professional qualities.

'He worked wonders with Mrs Calder,' Zena told Lee. 'She was still having a lot of trouble feeding her infant. I don't know how he did it.' She chuckled. 'I've never known a man, even an obstetrician, who has such empathy with mothers and babies! And he's a bachelor!'

The morning was well advanced before Lee encountered Trent.

She was supervising the return of a patient from Theatre after a myomectomy for the removal of uterine fibroids, when he came into the room.

'Lee!' His voice softened with concern. He came up to her, clasping her shoulders and peering anxiously into her face. 'How are you?'

She turned quickly. He was still wearing a green theatre gown and its colour seemed to emphasise his dark hair and eyes, the strong bones in his face. 'If I've said "I'm fine" once this morning, I've said it two dozen times. It's nice that everyone is so concerned about me, but really, I am OK. It was only a dose of flu.'

His eyes chided her. 'You know it was more than that.'

She shrugged. 'Shock too, but I'm over it now, Trent. Really. I'm all under control.' The way her heart was suddenly racing put the lie to that, and annoyed her. She must allow no feelings, except perhaps gratitude, to colour her relationship with Trent.

He glanced at the patient and walked over to the bed. 'How are you feeling, Mrs Price? A bit groggy, I expect. That's the anaesthetic.' The patient smiled and murmured something Lee did not catch. Trent clasped Mrs Price's hand. 'No, Sharon, it wasn't necessary to do a hysterectomy,' he reassured her gently. 'We were able to remove the fibroids without needing to do that, I'm pleased to say. In a little while it'll be perfectly all right for you to have a baby.'

The look of relief on the young woman's face was profound.

As they left the room, Trent said, 'She's a lucky lady. We had a little trouble with bleeding, so keep a sharp watch for any signs of haemorrhaging. We have a supply of cross-matched blood just in case. And if there's any abdominal distension or sign of paralytic ileus, let me know at once. We don't want toxaemia ruining all our good work and that young woman's future.'

'You've had a busy morning in Theatre,' Lee observed.

He nodded. 'I'll check the others. I like to have a reassuring word as soon after they're back in the wards as possible.'

Lee approved of that. 'Any difficult ops?' she asked.

'No. Pretty plain sailing really. Apart from Sharon Price, nothing that worried me, but of course we won't know for sure until all the path reports are back.'

They went into the next room, where three of the four patients had returned from surgery that morning and were in various stages of recovering from the anaesthetic. Trent spoke to each of them, ran his eye over their charts and seemed satisfied with most of the post-operation observations. One middle-aged woman's condition caused him concern, however.

'Mrs Grey's blood-pressure's a little too high,' he commented. 'What's she on? Aldomet? If there's no change at the next obs, let me know. We may have to increase the dosage or switch to another drug.'

He tossed a few other instructions at Lee which she jotted on her clipboard. He had a knack, she realised as the round progressed, of telling nursing staff what to do while sounding more as though he was reassuring patients than giving orders. She didn't find him either overbearing or humourless.

Their task finished, Lee would have left him, but Trent said, 'Come along to my office. There are a few things I want to talk to you about.'

When they were alone, he studied her for a moment, then said, 'You still look pale.' He reached out and pulled down her lower lids, frowning slightly, then he took her pulse. 'I think you'd better have a general check-up,' he advised. 'I suggest you go along and see Dr Ransome as soon as you can.'

'No, Trent, really, I'm all right. . .' Lee protested.

His gaze was stern, his voice firm. 'You'll do as I say, Sister Dennison.' He left her and picked up the phone. 'I'll make an appointment for you right now. You need a tonic to build you up after the flu.'

Lee rebelled a little at his high-handedness, but she did not continue her protest. She could see that it would be useless. Dr Allingham was clearly used to getting his own way.

The appointment was made for that afternoon around the time she would be finishing her shift. 'Was there something else?' asked Lee, as Trent put the phone down. 'You said you had a few things to discuss.' She added, 'Bryce told me you wanted a staff meeting soon to discuss the new department.'

'Quite right, but I thought we two would mull over a few points first.' He grinned conspiratorially at her. 'Consolidate our forces, you might say.'

Lee grinned back. 'What makes you think I'll be on your side?'

'I don't, but I always try to get redheads on my side! Otherwise they make formidable opponents!'

She laughed, more at ease now. 'Fire away, then.'

He perched on the edge of the desk. 'Firstly, the present set-up is untenable, having obstetrics and gynaecology combined. I want them separated. It's impossible for one charge nurse to cope with both sets of wards.' The dark eyes queried her. 'Would you agree with that?'

Lee nodded. 'Yes. With the volume of patient care increasing, we do have a problem apportioning staff. As Shearwater's population has grown, so has the need for medical services.'

'Good. I'm glad you agree.' He tapped his palm with a pen. 'You'll have a choice, of course, as to which area you would prefer.'

'Obstets,' Lee said without hesitation. 'I didn't do midwifery for a hobby.'

'That's fine. Now, as I see it. . .'

For half an hour, Trent outlined his general plan for the running of the two sections of the new department, and showed Lee on the plans how he envisaged the layout of wards, operating-rooms and facilities. Lee pored over the plans laid out across his desk, delighted to be having input into the new development, and eager to make suggestions of her own.

'No, no,' she objected when he pointed to the designated position for the sluice-room. 'That's too far away.' She lifted her eyes and smiled teasingly at him. 'It's easy to see you've never had to carry bedpans!'

'What's wrong with exercise?' he teased back. 'It'd do you lot good.'

'Come off it,' she protested. 'We're run off our feet as it is.'

'All right,' he agreed, jotting a query in the margin. 'We'll ask the plumbers to look into it.'

He agreed to investigate several other queries she had, and, absorbed by her enthusiasm for the project,

Lee forgot for a time that Trent was anything more in her life than just a senior colleague.

'OK, I think that'll do for now,' Trent said at last, and reached across to roll up the plans.

Lee reached out at the same time to stop a pen falling on to the floor, and their sudden opposite movements made their heads bump together.

'Oh, sorry!' Lee's hand flew to her forehead. Their faces were close, so close she could see the tiny darker flecks in his smoky grey irises, and for a moment there was a shocked silence. Then Trent let go of the plan and it cracked loudly as it rolled up of its own accord. He cupped Lee's face in his hands and touched her lips with his.

'Lee, how can you not remember?'

Lee felt the heat of sexual tension racing through her. How could she not remember indeed! She remembered only too vividly that night when Shannon had been conceived.

Trent's fingers crept around her neck caressingly, sending shocks down her spine that set off every alarm bell in her body.

'I remember,' she said, freezing her words, 'and I'm not in the running for a repeat performance, Trent. We're just colleagues now, and I wish you'd remember *that*.' She turned abruptly away from him and walked rapidly out of his office.

CHAPTER FOUR

'AND make sure you keep a check on Sharon Price's bowel movements,' Lee reminded Jennie Forrest, before she knocked off on Friday night. 'Alert Dr Allingham immediately if there's any concern.'

Jennie, the nurse taking over from Lee, nodded as she made notes of Lee's instructions.

Lee was glad she had not worked a whole week. It had been a hectic three days and she was tired. Although she hated to admit it, she still had a lingering weariness as a result of her bout of flu. Because Trent had insisted, she had submitted herself to examination by Dr Ransome, the hospital's senior physician, and had collected her bottle of tonic from Pharmacy. She planned to spend Saturday, at least, in bed.

It did not work out quite as she intended. Staying in bed after eight was not her style, and she felt guilty. By ten she was down in the garage discussing with Len the cost of some new brake-testing equipment. A snazzy red sports car zoomed in and an immaculately groomed woman got out. Lee wished she could look as elegant in white stirrup pants, emerald shirt and wrap-around sunglasses.

'Hello there,' the woman said, pushing her sunglasses up over her forehead on to glossy dark brown hair which framed a perfectly made up face.

'Is it just petrol you need?' Lee enquired.

'I stopped for directions, but I suppose I might as well fill up.'

'Where are you heading for?' asked Lee.

The woman treated her to a long, very penetrating appraisal. 'Are you Lee Dennison?' Her voice had an attractive husky tone.

Len had melted away. 'Yes?' Lee's answer was a query.

'Trent told me to stop here to ask the way,' the glamorous customer explained. 'He said it might be difficult to find Hilsborough.'

'Oh, it isn't at all.' Lee pointed in the direction of the house. 'You just go straight through the town and up the hill. You can't miss it.' One of his women friends, she surmised. Well, she had to admit he had taste.

The woman laughed. 'Trent knows my sense of direction is non-existent. He'd expect me to get lost.' She surveyed Lee with interest. 'By the way, I'm Francine Kennedy. I'm an interior designer—friend of Trent's. I'm down for a few days to look the place over. He said you had some brilliant ideas about how the house should be renovated.'

'Me? I just suggested he keep the colonial style,' Lee said, a little awed by the woman's poise and elegance. 'It's a splendid example of Victorian architecture. It would be a shame to modernise it too much.' She filled the car's tank. Francine Kennedy was the kind of woman people automatically did things for, even when she didn't need it, and probably didn't want them to. Especially men, Lee thought. Maybe especially Trent.

'He seemed to set great store by your opinions,' Francine said, her appraisal unrelenting. She waved a hand expansively, 'I must admit I'm amazed at Trent coming back here. I honestly can't imagine him living here permanently. It doesn't seem like his kind of place at all.' She laughed. 'No offence intended. But for

Trent. . .? Somehow I don't see it. He'll do the place up, and then sell it.'

Lee forbore to comment on what Trent might or might not do, although she was inclined to agree with Francine. As she screwed the cap back on the tank, she had a moment of envy. Francine was so elegant, the kind of woman who probably never bought a thing that didn't have a designer label. She probably didn't have, and never wore, old clothes. And she was lovely, so subtly made up, so classy, so—well, Trent's kind of woman.

After lunch, feeling weary, Lee stretched out on her bed and tried to sleep. Dr Ransome had told her to get as much rest as possible. But she had barely closed her eyes when Michael arrived, and after a swim in the motel pool they ended up going out for dinner.

Lee got up late on Sunday, feeling jaded. She put the 'CLOSED' notice with the emergency number, Len's, up on the service bay and checked the pumps before setting off to see Shannon. By the time she reached the Morrises' farm, she had perked up considerably and after lunch enjoyed a long ride with Shannon, who was developing into a very skilled horsewoman. We both like power and speed, Lee reflected in amusement, but she prefers horseflesh and I prefer machinery.

It was a perfect day. Shannon was full of her visit the previous day to a wildlife sanctuary, her new teacher at school, and, as they talked and laughed, Lee's loneliness was temporarily assuaged. The house behind the garage seemed very empty now her father was gone, she realised, especially at night. Her longing to have Shannon to live with her had deepened even more lately.

* * *

On Monday morning Lee's alarm called her as usual, and by seven-thirty she was at the hospital.

'How's Mrs Price?' was her first enquiry of the night staff going off.

'Her temp's up a bit,' the night nurse told her.

Sharon Price was more than just feverish, she was in real distress, and Lee was glad she had elected to see her first on her round.

'I think we'd better get Dr Allingham to look at you,' she told the anxious patient.

He came immediately. He was not pleased. 'You're supposed to let me know the minute any complication arises,' he rebuked sharply, drawing Lee aside.

'I'm not here at weekends,' she reminded him.

He glared as though that were a shortcoming. 'But I was! Why didn't someone tell me?'

'Obviously they didn't think it was that serious,' Lee defended.

His expression was furious. 'Then perhaps you'd better educate them! Paralytic ileus is a serious condition. Intestinal obstruction in a patient who's recently had abdominal surgery can be fatal.' He returned to the bedside and examined the patient methodically, then rapped out, 'I want pethidine, and a Miller Abbott tube—or whatever you have—for gastro-intestinal decompression. Now! I want an IV straight away, and make a note, nothing by mouth until I say so!'

'Yes, Doctor,' Lee said automatically. She felt to blame, even though she had not been there and it was not her fault that Sharon Price had been left to develop an advanced condition that was serious. She raced off to carry out Trent's instructions and muster assistance.

After that crisis had been dealt with, things were quiet in the wards. But the calm was not to last long.

Lee was writing up some case notes when the phone rang and Trent was telling her that there was an RTA being admitted, and one of the victims was pregnant, probably close to delivery time.

'Get ready,' he rapped out. 'They'll be bringing her straight to you. I'll be with you in a couple of minutes.'

And he was. Lee stood by his side as the orderlies transferred the inert patient to the delivery table. Her head and one arm had been heavily bandaged and a drip was being held high by a nurse. Lee pushed a stand into position and hooked the drip up, while Trent questioned the doctor who had come with the patient about what treatment she had already received in Casualty.

His examination was swift and thorough and his expression grim. 'We'll have to hurry if we're going to save them both,' he said. He looked hard at Lee for a moment. 'I'd like you to scrub for me, Lee.'

'Me? But. . .'

'Half the theatre staff is down with the flu. I need someone competent. Don't argue, woman!'

'I haven't scrubbed for ages,' she protested, aghast. Why on earth would he think she would be more competent than any of the regular theatre nurses?

Trent's gaze was dark, determined. 'I said don't argue! This is a matter of life and death and I want someone I know I can rely on.'

Lee swallowed hard. There wasn't time to argue—or to feel flattered. Once more she raced off to do as he wanted, leaving the orderlies and another nurse to transport the patient to the operating-room and Trent to organise cross-matching of blood and transfusion equipment.

Within minutes Lee was gloved and gowned and

checking the instruments on the tray beside the operating table. Trent was listening for the baby's heartbeat, while the anaesthetist prepared the patient for what would be a delicate and possibly dangerous operation. The young woman very likely had internal as well as external injuries. Her pulse was erratic and her blood-pressure was giving cause for concern. Lee glanced at Trent, knowing it was going to be touch and go, and that all his surgical skill and that of the surgeon assisting him would be needed.

'I can't detect any heartbeat in the baby,' Trent finally said, grim-faced. 'But that doesn't mean. . .' He broke off as the anaesthetist called for his attention. There was a rapid consultation, then he turned back to Lee and nodded at the second surgeon who had arrived. 'OK, let's start.'

It was one of the most difficult operations Lee had ever assisted at. The baby was dead, and for long, long minutes after it had been delivered it seemed the mother would die too. As Trent and the other surgeon had suspected, her internal injuries were serious, and it took some time to repair tissue and staunch the haemorrhaging. Even when the operation was finished and the woman wheeled away to Intensive Care, there was no expression of relief or confidence from the participants. It was still touch and go, and would be for some hours. Lee felt drained, and the faces of the rest of the team, their reluctance to discuss the operation, indicated that they felt the same way.

As she was tossing her gown into the laundry bin, Lee felt a hand on her shoulder.

'Thanks, Lee. You did a great job.' Trent was not smiling, but she was touched by his thanks. He looked strained and weary and the lines around his eyes still showed tension. The level of concentration required of them all had been at the limits.

'Do you think she'll pull through?' asked Lee.

'I don't know.' He grasped her arm. 'We need some coffee. You look whacked.' A corner of his mouth lifted slightly. 'I know I feel it.'

Lee automatically placed her hand over his in a brief expression of comfort. Surgeons seldom admitted how they really felt about fighting to save lives, especially to nurses.

There was a coffeemaker in the surgeons' room. No one else was there. The surgeon who had assisted had gone to check on the condition of the other accident victims. Trent handed Lee a cup of coffee. She asked, 'Any idea what happened?'

'The accident, you mean?'

She nodded.

'Some lunatic who forgot to look right at the intersection by the water tower. She was taking her two older kids to school, and now they're all here, as well as the lunatic.'

'Alive?' Lee placed her cup of coffee on the table. It was too hot to drink.

He nodded. 'One of the children has a broken collarbone and lacerations, the other concussion and a broken leg. The other driver was thrown clear and has spinal injuries. We'll probably have to fly him up to Melbourne.'

Lee covered her face with her hands. 'It's awful. I hate RTAs. To see people so smashed up. . .' She looked up at Trent, anguished. 'We couldn't have saved the baby, could we?' Whenever a patient in whose care she had been involved died, Lee always wondered if they had done all they could, even when she knew they had.

'No.' He added slowly, 'And I'm glad we couldn't. With those sort of injuries, he wouldn't have had any sort of quality of life.'

Lee felt the strain of the past couple of hours telling. She swayed slightly, and Trent caught her arm. 'Hey, you're not going to pass out on me, are you?'

'No. . .' Lee took a deep breath and then in spite of her effort to keep control of herself, she bent her head and wept on his shoulder. 'Think how she's going to feel when she wakes up and finds out she's lost her baby!' Suddenly she felt deeply for the young woman, who was still unconscious, unknowing.

Trent tightened his arm around her. 'We did our best, Lee. And her other children are alive and will recover. She'll be thankful for that.'

'I know. . .it's just that. . .' She couldn't say that when you had a child of your own, you identified more keenly with other people's tragedies.

There was no one else in the room. It was quiet save for the faint hum of the air-conditioning and the intermittent hissing of the coffeemaker. Trent bent his head and touched his lips to Lee's, teasing them a little, then kissing her hard and long, more from release of tension than with passion, and she let herself enjoy the passage of strength from him to her. He was as irresistible to her as he'd been before, she realised, hearing warning bells through the fog in her tired mind. She pulled away, and he looked quizzical.

'What's up?' he asked.

Lee shrugged. 'You shouldn't have done that. I wish you wouldn't.' She moved away and snatched up her coffee, gulping it. 'The poor father will be distraught. I wonder if anyone has told him yet.'

'I expect so. They locate people pretty quickly.'

Lee looked at him and heard herself saying recklessly, 'You spend your life dealing with mothers and babies. Haven't you ever wanted to be a father yourself?'

A half-smile moved his lips. Then it became a short burst of laughter. 'Not really. I don't think somehow it's a role I would feel comfortable with, or be good at.'

The following Saturday, Lee took Shannon up to Melbourne as it was her birthday. She borrowed Callie's car, as she never went too far afield on the motorbike and there was no way she would ever have let Shannon ride pillion, the way she once used to with Trent.

As she arrived at the farm, Shannon ran to meet her. 'Happy birthday, darling,' said Lee, hugging and kissing her. 'How does it feel to be eleven?'

'Fantastic!' laughed Shannon, her eyes widening at the large parcel Lee had extricated from her carrier. She hugged it to her. 'What is it?'

'Open it and see! Something you've been hinting for.'

Shannon giggled. 'I know! I know!' She raced on ahead into the house just as Callie came out to greet Lee.

'She's so excited,' Callie said, with affection. 'If your present is what I think it is, she'll be over the moon.'

'I only hope it fits,' said Lee.

A few minutes later Shannon swaggered in, resplendent in jodhpurs, jacket, a hard hat and riding boots. 'Hey, you guys, look at me!'

Callie's husband, Nick, whistled. 'You'd better not grow out of that too soon,' he teased.

'How's the fit, Shan?' Lee asked anxiously.

Shannon twirled. 'Great. I suppose Aunty Callie gave you all the measurements. I had a hunch that was what she was taping me for, but she said it was for my new school uniform.'

'That too,' said Callie. She inspected Shannon's outfit. 'Very nice—good quality. You'll have to take good care of it, Shan.'

'Like not falling off your horse till you spread a tarp,' joked Ned, Callie's teenage son.

'Off you go and change,' Lee said to Shannon. 'You can't go to Melbourne dressed like that.'

'Come and see what else I got.' Shannon tugged her mother off to look at her birthday presents.

All the way to Melbourne, Shannon chattered about school, the pony club, the Morrises and a host of other things. She seldom asked about Lee's own life, and today was no exception. Eleven-year-old girls' interests did tend to centre on school and pop stars, and, with Shannon, horses were her current passion. As usual Shannon asked a couple of questions about the hospital and then was off on another tack. Lee didn't mind. Her lack of curiosity about her mother's life in Shearwater meant Lee did not have to prevaricate. Shannon had only once or twice shown any inclination to go there, and when Lee had made excuses, she had not persisted. Evidently it sounded like a pretty dull place to her and she was glad not to have to endure going there just to please her mother.

Melbourne was a different story. Shannon loved going to Melbourne, and Lee had brought her up for a treat every birthday when she'd lived there.

'I wish you still lived here,' Shannon said as the skyline came into view. 'Where are we going first?'

'The new Melbourne Central complex. It'll take all

the time we've got to see it all. There's a big department store, lots of small shops and restaurants, and a host of other things. You remember the old shot tower? It's been preserved under a glass cone inside the building, and there's a very interesting clock near it. I'm not going to tell you any more—you can see for yourself.'

Lee let Shannon choose a restaurant for lunch, and, after they had window-shopped for a while, Shannon rushed around taking photographs with the new camera the Morrises had given her.

'We must ask someone to take the two of us together,' she said finally, looking round for a likely candidate.

It was then that Lee, following her gaze, saw Trent. He was walking towards them, casually looking around, a carrier bag from a well-known men's store in his hand. For a moment Lee thought he would pass without noticing them, and she held her breath.

He might have done, if Shannon hadn't picked on him to take the photograph she wanted. She made a beeline for him, waving her camera, and boldly asking him to oblige. Lee saw Trent look startled, then he smiled indulgently down at the little girl, murmured something and glanced up looking for her mother. Their eyes met, and Lee swallowed hard as she saw the surprise, then pleasure in his. He hadn't connected her yet with the child.

'Lee!' he exclaimed. 'This is a surprise.' He indicated Shannon with a glance at her. 'Just a minute, I've got to take a picture for this young lady.'

Shannon stared. 'Hey, do you guys know each other?'

A strange expression crossed Trent's face as he looked from one to the other.

Lee said with an effort, 'Yes. This is Dr Allingham, darling. He works at the hospital too.' She then had to look at Trent. His face was a study in incredulity. 'Trent, you've just met my daughter Shannon,' she said.

A host of expressions flicked across his face, but he decided it was not the moment to ask questions. He merely held out his hand to Shannon and said, 'How do you do, Shannon? I'm pleased to meet you.'

'It's amazing!' Shannon was saying. 'Imagine, Mum, I picked out someone you actually know. In all these hundreds of people I picked someone you *know*!'

Lee forced herself to smile. 'I'm as flabbergasted as you are, darling,' she said. 'It's truly amazing.'

Trent's shock was profound, but he recovered himself a little and endeavoured to act normally. 'Must have been a special kind of magnetism,' he joked. 'Now, shall I take that photo for you, Shannon?'

'Yes, please. Can you take one with the shot tower in the background, and one with the clock?' She turned and pointed to the giant replica of a fob watch which hung above them. As she did so it struck the hour, and Shannon gaped as the bottom of the clock was lowered to reveal plastic birds mechanically flapping their wings as cherubs played trumpets and the strains of 'Waltzing Matilda', together with bird whistles, entranced the gathering crowd.

Trent glanced at Lee and whispered, 'Did you ever see such kitsch?'

She gave him a mock-reproving look. 'Shannon thinks it's fantastic. And so does everyone else! This is fantasyland, Trent!'

Trent just rolled his eyes and smiled, and there was an instant of rapport between them before Shannon turned round wide-eyed at the close of the performance to exclaim her wonder. Trent positioned them for a photo, and Lee had some difficulty keeping a smile pinned on her face. This was the most embarrassing situation she had been in so far with Trent. No, more than embarrassing, it was agonising.

'W-what are you doing in Melbourne?' she managed to ask as he handed the camera back to Shannon.

He swung the bag he was holding. 'I needed a few things, and as one of my colleagues from Sydney is here for the weekend, we met for lunch. I'm just browsing now before I catch the train home.'

'You came by train?' Lee was surprised.

'I wasn't sure about parking. It's always hell in Sydney. Anyway, I rather like trains. It's more relaxing than driving.' Shannon had moved off to look at something else that had caught her eye, so Trent said, half reproachfully, 'You didn't tell me you had a daughter.'

'No. I—I haven't told anyone in Shearwater.'

His eyes were dark, intense. 'Max knew, though?'

She looked away. 'No. I never told my parents. I couldn't. . .' She choked on the words. Confessions in public places were horrible. 'Trent, I'd rather not talk about it. Not here.' Not anywhere!

'No, of course not.' He rested a hand on her arm. 'Sorry.'

Shannon rushed over to them. 'Come and look, Mum. They've got the cutest little pottery animals in that shop. The horses are fantastic!'

Lee was grateful for the interruption. She glanced at Trent. 'She's at the age to be mad about horses!'

Shannon put in, 'Mum gave me the most fantastic

riding outfit.' She added ingenuously, 'It's my birthday. I'm eleven.'

Trent was captivated by her. 'Congratulations. Eleven is the age I'd like to have been all my life.'

Shannon shot him a look that said she wasn't sure whether he was pulling her leg or not. They all went to look in the shop window, and Trent said, 'I was thinking about afternoon tea when I met you two. Would you like to join me?'

'Yes, please,' said Shannon at once, and Lee could hardly spoil what her daughter evidently regarded as a bonus treat.

It was an unnerving experience, though, sitting at a table having afternoon tea with her daughter and the father of her daughter. Would he guess? she thought with a kind of resignation. Would he realise that she had lied to him all those years ago? And if he did, what would he say?

Lee's thoughts were miles away when she suddenly heard Shannon saying to Trent, whom she had instantly regarded as an old friend, it seemed, 'You can come back with us if you like, Dr Allingham. Mum's got her bike at the Morrises'. You can ride pillion back to Shearwater!' She chuckled delightedly. 'It'll scare you silly, I expect. Mum's a real daredevil!' She grinned at her mother. 'Dr Allingham likes motorcycles, Mum.'

'Yes, I know,' said Lee, contemplating the prospect her daughter had described with some dismay. 'I think you'll be more comfortable by train,' she advised.

He disagreed. 'I think it sounds like an adventure not to be missed.'

'Well, if you want to risk your neck,' Lee said as lightly as she could. She glanced at her watch. 'We must be going soon. The car's in the car park down below.

Would you like to meet us there in a few minutes? Shannon and I have to go to the Ladies.'

As they went to find the Ladies, Shannon said, 'He's super, Mum. Is he your boyfriend?'

'No, he's just a doctor at the hospital.'

'He's nice,' said Shannon, and there was a faintly wistful note in her voice that jabbed straight at Lee's heart. Was Shannon reaching the age when the lack of a father was beginning to matter? She had always accepted Nick Morris as a father figure, but maybe she was now beginning to wonder about her real father. One day soon she was going to ask the kind of questions which Lee might feel she ought to answer truthfully.

Trent was waiting for them near the lifts. As Lee was unlocking the car he handed a small packet to Shannon. 'Happy birthday, Shannon.'

Her eyes widened. 'It's for me?'

'Anybody else around here having a birthday?' he said, feigning a visual search for them.

'You shouldn't have,' Lee scolded. 'She's spoiled enough already.'

'When a lovely young lady offers you a lift home,' he said, his eyes holding Lee's, 'it's only polite to give her a small gift.'

Shannon was carefully opening the packet. When the tiny, perfectly modelled piebald horse was revealed, she gave a shriek of delight. 'It's the one I said was just like my horse, Pastry!' She threw herself at Trent and kissed him. 'I wasn't hinting, truly. But thank you! Thank you! Thank you!'

Seeing him with his arms around his daughter made Lee flinch. Trent said, 'It was the smallest one in the shop. A mere token.' He smiled at Lee over the top of Shannon's head.

Lee forced herself to say, 'You still shouldn't have, but it was kind. I know she'll treasure it.' There was a hard lump in her throat and tears burned behind her eyes. Momentarily she longed to tell him that he had just given his first birthday gift to his daughter.

Shannon, who still seemed to have boundless energy, monopolised the conversation all the way home. Lee did not mind. It was her day, and she had a new, willing listener. Trent might not think he had the qualifications for fatherhood, but there was no doubt he was good with children as well as babies and their mums. His slightly wry brand of humour was a perfect foil for Shannon's exuberance, and he pulled her leg a lot, which she seemed to enjoy. But Trent didn't *want* to be a father. He valued his freedom too much, Lee knew. The road back seemed endless, and Lee was mostly silent, numbed by the awful irony of the situation.

When they arrived at the farm, there were explanations and introductions to make. Lee caught Callie giving her a questioning look that probably meant the same as Shannon's enquiry as to whether Trent was a boyfriend. Lee unobtrusively shook her head. They were persuaded to stay for tea, and left soon afterwards, before it was quite dark.

Ned Morris, who also rode a motorcycle, produced a spare helmet for Trent.

'You can ride pillion, if you like,' Trent said to Lee, as they prepared to leave.

She raised a teasing eyebrow. 'Afraid you won't look macho enough on the back?'

'No, I just want to feel your arms around my waist,' he countered, then added, 'I also want to feel the wind in my face and see a long stretch of road ahead. I haven't ridden any distance on a bike for years.'

'All right,' she said, straddling the pillion, 'I don't mind.'

Holding tightly to Trent, her cheek against his broad back, the wind whistling past her head, the verges a blur, Lee felt the same exhilaration as she had riding with him before. It wasn't just being on a powerful machine, it was because Trent's body was warm and vibrant under her encircling arms and she could feel his heartbeat through the taut muscles of his back. I still love him, she thought, with bleak despair.

At Hilsborough, as the motorcycle's engine died and Lee dismounted, she felt an acute sense of loss. It had been Shannon's day, but in a way hers too.

'Come in and have a coffee,' Trent invited, kicking the bike's stand into position.

'No, I think I'd better. . .'

He took her arm. 'It's not late.' He was smiling persuasively, and, because he had been kind to Shannon, she felt she couldn't be churlish.

'We didn't get much chance to talk,' he said, when they were drinking coffee in the drawing-room.

Lee was silent, fearful of what he might be going to say. He did not keep her waiting long. Watching her face, he said, 'You must have been very young when Shannon was born.'

She moistened her lips. 'Yes.'

'And not married.'

'No.' She stared at the carpet.

'Eleven years ago. It must have upset your nursing training.'

Lee could not bear to look at him. 'It had to be put on hold for a few months, that's all. They were very understanding.'

'So, if your parents didn't know, how did you manage?' He had difficulty keeping his voice level.

She told him about Callie. 'I don't know what I would have done without her.' She looked up and for a moment there was nothing but a painful eye contact between them, then Trent said,

'Shannon's my daughter, isn't she?'

'Yes.' Lee's voice was a whisper.

He reached out and grasped her wrist, gripping it hard until it hurt. She winced and he relaxed a little. 'You knew you were pregnant when I phoned you from Sydney, didn't you, but you said everything was OK?'

There was no point in pretending. 'I wasn't sure. I was still hoping it might be a false alarm.'

'Why didn't you tell me when you were sure?'

'Isn't it obvious?' she retorted. 'You'd have thought I was just trying to force you to marry me, maybe even trapped you. You were about to embark on a difficult and demanding career, later than most people. You didn't want a family hindering you. I didn't want you to marry me because you felt you had to. You would have resented that. Imagine what your parents would have said! And when I'd told you everything was OK, the relief in your voice was so plain. I just felt it would be better if you never knew.'

Lee looked down at her tightly twined hands. Remembering was almost more painful than she could bear. Trent had asked her to let him know her address and telephone number in Melbourne, so as soon as she had settled in she had written him a short note. A few weeks went by and she'd decided he didn't want to contact her, but one night she had picked up the phone in the flat she was sharing with two other girls and heard his voice. To her amazement, he was in Sydney and about to embark on the medical career he'd said he always wanted, but which she hadn't thought he was really serious about. It was why he hadn't rung before. 'I only got your note a few days ago,' he'd said, 'when some mail was sent on to me.'

Their conversation had been stilted, as though they hardly knew each other, and when Lee had realised that he was anxious about her because they'd made love with no protection, she hadn't the courage to tell him her fears. He had rung twice more, but Lee had faced the fact that, although he was concerned about her, he didn't love her. She loved him enough not to want to hinder his late-starting medical career with unwanted responsibilities, and being realistic, she'd known that Trent would never ask her to marry him unless he felt obliged. She didn't belong in his world and she was not going to force herself into it.

He said, 'What are we going to do?'

Lee looked up quickly, startled. 'Do?'

He leaned forward earnestly. 'We ought to get married.'

She leapt up. 'No! Don't be ridiculous, Trent.'

He rose too and laid a hand on her arm. 'Lee, think about it—please. You don't have to decide now. We'll talk about it later. When you're ready to.'

Lee stared at him. What he was suggesting was as impossible now as it had ever been, but her heart was leaping about in her chest like a mad thing.

'I'd better be going,' she muttered. 'Thanks for being nice to Shannon on her birthday.'

He didn't try to stop her. 'The pleasure was all mine,' he murmured.

CHAPTER FIVE

'PULMONARY embolus, I'm afraid,' said Trent in a tone that while deeply regretful did not convey his real feelings of helplessness.

Biting her lip, Lee drew the curtains around the bed. 'How can it happen. . .? So suddenly? She rang and said she wanted a bedpan, and when Rose got back. . .' Her voice broke and she shook her head in disbelief. 'I've never encountered that before. What should I have done?' Anguish clouded her eyes.

They were temporarily alone. Trent curled his fingers around her forearm and squeezed comfortingly. 'Lee, it wasn't your fault. You take too much responsibility. You can't be responsible for *everything*!'

She was too choked to reply. An hour ago she had been chatting to Emily Banks, who had had a hysterectomy that morning. The patient had been cheerful, relieved that the operation was over, and there had been no indication that her recovery was not proceeding normally. Or was there some sign the other nurses had missed, or more particularly that she, Lee, had missed?

Trent's fingers caressed her arm reassuringly. 'Lee, stop blaming yourself. You know what a pulmonary embolus is. You know that little can be done to save the patient once the blood supply to the lungs has been cut off. You know that as the blood clot passes through the heart it stimulates the vagus nerve and causes intensive peristalis, which makes the patient want a bedpan.'

His clinical explanation rammed her brain but did not dissolve her anguish. 'I know, I know, I know!' Lee did know, of course, but she felt a strong need to talk about it. 'She was unconscious by the time Rose reached her,' she said. 'Her pulse was faint and her temperature had fallen dramatically.'

'And you did exactly what you should have done. You called me,' said Trent. 'It wasn't your fault, Lee. There weren't necessarily any prior symptoms that might have alerted even a more experienced nurse than Rose.'

Lee glanced at the pretty floral curtains closed around the bed. They seemed inappropriately cheerful. 'It was so sudden. . .'

Still no one else had come in. Trent drew her close to comfort her. 'Lee, I feel as badly about it as you do. Nobody likes to lose a patient. But we did our best. We gave her oxygen. We tried morphine, we tried heparin, we tried everything. We're not miracle-workers.'

Lee rested her head on his shoulder. 'I know. . .' She didn't tell him that she had warmed immediately to Emily because she reminded her of her mother. He would think her sentimental. Nurses were not supposed to become involved.

He rocked her gently and she responded to his strength instinctively. The trouble was, she knew, she had never quite become used to people dying. To her nursing had always been a way of triumphing over accident and disease, and most of the time it was. When it wasn't, when someone died, Lee could not help feeling responsible. It haunted her for days afterwards.

'It's one of the tragedies of surgery,' Trent said in a grim tone. 'We're not infallible, Lee. There are some things we can't prevent. Unfortunately, because we have so much sophisticated technology these days, people think we can do anything, but sometimes we can't.'

She pulled away from him, ashamed of her weakness. 'I'd better go. Her husband will have to be told.'

He said, 'I'll do that.'

Lee gave him a grateful smile. 'Some people get all the unglamorous jobs,' she said lightly, in an attempt to sound in control of herself.

Fortunately for her, there was plenty to distract her that day. Mothers and babies to be discharged, new patients to be admitted. She spent her time flying from obstetric to gynaecological wards with the thought uppermost in her mind that the opening of the new wing could not be too soon.

One new admission was a rather sullen young woman who was obviously an unmarried mother. The baby was not due for a couple of weeks, but she had been admitted because of a kidney problem. She caused the nurses a great deal of inconvenience with her demands, she was rude and uncooperative, and out of earshot Zena threatened to spank her.

It was the first light moment in a hard day. Lee laughed. 'I'd like to see you try to spank a woman in advanced pregnancy!'

'Somebody should have done it ages ago,' said Zena. 'I'm not surprised she hasn't got a husband.'

'Don't be so judgemental!' Lee remonstrated.

Zena said darkly, 'You go and talk to her. And if I hear you've tipped her next urine sample over her head. . .!'

As soon as she had a free moment, Lee went. Rachel Armstrong was in a private room and her mother was with her. Lee, sensing a tense atmosphere, backed away. 'I'll come back later,' she began.

'No, stay, please, Sister,' said Mrs Armstrong. 'Perhaps you can help talk some sense into my daughter.' She looked Lee over with a haughty glance. Her demeanour, her voice, her expensive clothes, explained her better than words.

Lee did not know anyone called Armstrong. She guessed that they were holiday people, one of the growing number of city people who had holiday homes in Shearwater, and yachts, and Porsches in the driveways of their trendy residences. That Rachel was having her baby in Shearwater rather than Toorak or Hawthorn was no coincidence. Times might have changed, but babies born to teenagers out of wedlock were no more welcomed in some families now than they had ever been. Lee suspected that Mrs Armstrong was probably more concerned about the reflection on her of Rachel's pregnancy than Rachel's own welfare.

'Leave it, Mum,' the pale girl in the bed said irritably. 'I've already made up my mind—I told you. I wish you'd go. I'm tired.' Under the stress, she was pretty, Lee thought, too pretty perhaps for her own good.

Mrs Armstrong was not unwilling. She rose, but made her position clear to Lee before she left. 'Rachel's seventeen,' she said. 'She's clever and intelligent and could have a good career. Her father and I want her to go to university and study law, so we agreed it would be best to have the baby adopted. At first she was sensible and agreed, but now she's changed her mind and wants to bring it up herself, which is ridiculous. Her father and I don't feel obliged to raise some irresponsible young student's bastard—it will ruin

Rachel's career, and her chances of marrying well—so if she's going to be stubborn about it. . .'

Lee swallowed a sharp retort. How could anyone still be so Victorian? So unfeeling? A wave of remembered anguish washed over her. Mrs Armstrong reminded her of Mrs Allingham. Looking at the girl in the bed, she said quietly, 'We'll have a chat later, perhaps?' The look she received was as sullen as ever, but Lee was sure she detected a faint gratitude because she had refused to discuss the situation in front of Rachel's mother.

But what was she going to say to the girl? Later when she went back to see Rachel, she was still burning to tell her not to be intimidated, that if she wanted her baby she should keep it, or ever after regrets might spoil her happiness. It was probably just as well, she thought, that Rachel was asleep. Persuading the girl one way or the other was not part of her duty.

But Trent seemed to think it was. He strolled into her office not long before she was due to go off duty. He perched on a corner of the desk and eyed her steadily for a moment or two. As she did whenever she saw him alone these days, Lee tensed, wondering if he was going to bring up the subject of marriage again. But so far he hadn't.

Trent had great difficulty in keeping silent. He was kicking himself again for being too precipitate, and had decided he must let Lee think about it, all in her own good time. Besides, he needed time to think himself. Discovering he had an eleven-year-old daughter had been a profound shock.

Now he said, 'Lee, I think you could help Rachel. You must know better than anyone how she must feel.'

Lee bit her lip. The memory was painful.

'You had the guts to go it alone,' Trent reminded her, 'but, like you, Rachel needs some moral support. She needs to know someone else has been through the mill too. I know her situation is different because she hasn't kept it a secret from her parents, but that's still making it difficult for her. Maybe she's wishing now she hadn't told them.'

'Sometimes I wish I had,' Lee said softly, 'but every time I made up my mind to tell them, I got cold feet, and the longer you leave the telling the harder it becomes. In the end I was afraid of the shock Dad would get if I told him. I didn't want him to have another stroke.'

Trent nodded. 'But he had one anyway.'

'Maybe it was wrong of me not to let him know he had a granddaughter and Shannon she had a grandfather.'

Trent gave a wry little smile. 'That's you, Lee, always worrying whether you've done the right thing.'

She tilted her chin. 'I suppose you're always sure that what you're doing is the best course.'

To her surprise he said, 'Of course I'm not.' He drew in a deep breath and let it out slowly. 'Lee, believe me, for years I agonised because I'd gone against my father's wishes to become a doctor. It caused a lot of heartache.' He paused, his face showing the pain of recollection. He said slowly, 'The only time I saw him after the day he threw me out was at my mother's funeral, and he didn't even speak to me. Do you think I don't have regrets?'

Lee was shocked. 'Your father threw you out?' She had not imagined Trent's leaving home to be like that, and found it hard to believe. 'What happened?'

Trent clasped his hands behind his head. 'When I

finally broke the news to my father that I intended to become a doctor whether he liked it or not, he was furious. So was my mother. Who was going to carry on the family tradition at Hilsborough if I quit? I was their only child. I was cruel, they said, irresponsible. We argued, and finally, in the heat of the moment, I told them I didn't care about Hilsborough, that all that mattered to me was that I did what I wanted to do, medicine. I couldn't afford to waste any more time trying to do what they wanted when my heart wasn't in it.'

'I can imagine how upset they must have been,' said Lee.

He laughed harshly. 'It was like sacrilege—the unforgivable insult. We had the row to end all rows, the day after my twenty-first birthday. Dad told me to pack my bags and go and never come back. I hadn't expected that, and I was devastated, but also determined and proud. I flung some belongings into a suitcase and stormed out of the house saying nothing would persuade me to come back, ever.'

'What about your mother?'

He said sadly, 'She would never go against my father's wishes.' He gave a rueful smile. 'She was shocked. She begged me to think it over and come back when we'd all had time to cool down, but I knew it would be no use. My father would never change. Hilsborough had been his life, his father's and his grandfather's and great-grandfather's lives. To have a son who wasn't interested in raising stud rams and making smart investments on the Stock Exchange was untenable. He never came to terms with my disloyalty, never forgave me for the insult.'

Lee was astounded at his revelation. 'But in spite of it, he still left you everything.'

'No one was more surprised than me,' Trent told her. 'But there was only a distant cousin otherwise, and maybe it was his posthumous attempt to bring me back, to Hilsborough, if not to be a grazier like him.'

'Which it did!' Lee added, 'I'm afraid you've been sadly misjudged by all of us.'

'It doesn't matter.'

'Why didn't you tell me,' she asked, 'when you phoned me from Sydney that time? I never dreamed you could have left home like that.'

He shrugged again. 'I was still too churned up to talk about it, and why should I have worried you with my problems, anyway? You didn't worry me with yours.' Their eyes met for a moment, before he went on, 'I don't know why I'm telling you now. We've got off the track a bit. We were talking about Rachel. I think you could help her, Lee.'

Lee was doubtful. 'I had a short conversation with the mother. Not a very sympathetic person, and the father sounds worse.'

He reached out and covered her hand briefly with his. 'Would you advise Rachel to keep her baby?'

'It's her choice,' she said. 'It has to be her decision. I don't think I should advise. . .'

'Because you're biased?'

'It's not my role,' she insisted. 'She should see a counsellor.'

Trent leaned closer across the desk, his eyes very steady, very penetrating. 'Lee, she's going to have her life mapped out for her by selfish parents who have no appreciation of what kind of person she really is, or sympathy for what she wants to do with her life, just the way it nearly was for me, could have been for you. Help her—unofficially, as a friend.' He added in a flat tone, 'One day she might want to acknowledge the father and he might be glad to know.'

Lee firmed her lips and took a deep breath. 'All right, I'll try. You're nothing if not unorthodox, Trent!'

'There are some things I'm pretty orthodox about,' he said, his mood changing abruptly, 'and this is one of them.' He pulled her into his arms and kissed her lightly, then with increasing fervour until, alarmed, she pulled back.

'Trent. . .please! Someone might come in.'

He tilted her chin and brushed a finger lightly across her mouth. 'Then we'll have to find a less public rendezvous.'

'No!' Lee spoke sharply. 'No, Trent. Please leave me alone.'

His mouth hardened. 'This man, Michael Farrow, is he important in your life?'

'How do you know about Michael?'

He smiled thinly. 'I'm a curious person, Lee. I ask questions. Well, is he?'

'Maybe.'

When Lee set off for the Morrises' farm on Sunday, she had only ridden a couple of hundred yards when her motorcycle suddenly coughed, choked and stopped. It refused to re-start and she was faced with having to wheel the heavy machine all the way back to the garage.

'Damn!' she exclaimed. Now she would have to ring and tell them she would be late. Providing she could fix whatever was wrong with the bike. . . She trudged slowly back. A hundred yards from the garage, a horn tooted behind her, and glancing round she saw Trent's car. He stopped and jumped out.

'What's the trouble?'

'Broken down,' she muttered through her teeth.

'Where were you off to? To see Shannon?'

Lee nodded.

'I'll take you,' Trent offered. He grabbed hold of the bike's handlebars. 'Let's get the bike back to the garage. Here, let me. . . You follow in the car.'

Before she could protest, he had commandeered the bike and was wheeling it the rest of the way to the garage. Lee cruised along behind in the Merc and put the machine away.

'Don't worry, I won't hang around,' he said, as she got into the passenger-seat and he slid behind the car's steering-wheel. 'I'll take myself off somewhere for lunch and pick you up at whatever time you say.'

'But you'd like to see Shannon?'

'Of course,' he said quietly, 'but not if it's going to upset you.'

She didn't promise. 'Do you remember the way?' she asked.

'I think so.'

'Surely you had something to do today,' Lee suggested. 'This must be taking you out of your way.'

'Nothing special,' he said. 'I just thought I'd get away for a few hours, have lunch somewhere and maybe visit a winery.' He glanced at her. 'There's one near your friends' place, I believe, which has a recommended restaurant.'

'That's Magpie Ridge.' Lee's gaze met his and she felt a wave of heat engulf her. She couldn't let him do that! 'You can't do that,' she said. 'You must have lunch with us. Callie won't mind, she always has stacks of food.'

He smiled gratefully. 'Thanks.'

Shannon was surprised and delighted to see Trent again, and she was determined to monopolise him. After extracting a promise that he would ride with them during the afternoon, she carted him off immediately after lunch to look at a sheepdog bitch who had just had puppies.

Lee and Callie cleared away the lunch dishes and washed up. Stacking plates on the drainer, Callie finally brought Trent into the conversation. She did not beat about the bush.

'He's Shannon's father, isn't he?'

Lee flushed deeply. 'It didn't take you long to guess.'

Callie grinned. 'I'm good at putting two and two together. But don't worry, I won't let on, and I doubt very much if it would occur to Nick or the kids in a thousand years. Does Trent know?'

Lee sighed. 'Yes. As soon as he knew her age, he suspected.' Since there was no point in concealing it now, she told Callie the rest of the story, and why she had not told Trent when she discovered she was pregnant.

'Shannon seems to have taken to him,' Callie observed.

'Yes—it's uncanny. She picked him out of a crowd to take a photo of us, as though she knew. . .'

'Fate,' said Callie, with a sly glance at Lee.

'Coincidence,' insisted Lee.

Callie observed thoughtfully, 'I dare say she'd like a father she doesn't have to share with four other kids. Especially her real father.' She looked at Lee expectantly. 'He's not married, is he?'

'No, but what you're thinking isn't possible, Callie,' Lee said. 'We're worlds apart. It wouldn't work. Besides, he has a very glamorous girlfriend, probably several. The one I know is organising the refurbishing of his house, and she's exactly his type. I'm not. I couldn't marry him just to give Shannon her real name. Nothing's changed.'

Callie cocked an eyebrow at her. 'Has he suggested it?'

'Yes. But that's only because he feels he ought to.'

Callie wiped her hands on a towel. 'I'm not surprised you fell for him, Lee. He's very good-looking. And nice.'

Lee decided to put an end to it. 'So's Michael,' she said defensively, and a little too loudly, 'and Michael will make a very good husband.'

When she straightened up, Trent was standing in the doorway. He had probably heard her last remark.

'Ready?' he asked. 'Your mount is waiting, ma'am!'

Shannon was eager to show Trent the entire farm. She and Trent rode side by side most of the time, while Lee brought up the rear. As they usually did on hot days, they stopped at the dam in the shade of some trees, tethered the horses and went for a swim. Lee caught Trent's eye as she stripped off to the bathing suit she had worn under her shirt and jeans, and there was a glint in his that made her look away quickly. There was deeper water than the water in the dam.

Shannon swung on the rope that hung from a tree branch that jutted out over the water, jumped in and dared Trent to follow. Of course he did, executing a very stylish dive from the branch, to applause from Shannon, while Lee followed a little more sedately from the bank. There was a great deal of horseplay, with shrieks of delight from Shannon, who was clearly in her element.

Lee swam a little, then climbed out and sat on the bank watching Trent and Shannon race each other. It was almost as though they were a family. 'We *are* a family,' she whispered. But she mustn't indulge in wishful thinking. Even if he wouldn't admit it, Trent was merely being kind, indulging an eleven-year-old, even basking in her attention perhaps, carried away by the novelty of discovering himself father to a beautiful daughter. But it wouldn't last. It was clear that so far he had deliberately avoided the responsibilities of fatherhood, and Lee was sure she was not going to inflict them on him, by taking advantage of his sense of obligation. She only needed to remind herself of his relief when she had said, 'I'm fine, Trent. There's nothing to worry about.'

They left soon after tea, and Lee was hardly surprised when Trent, following a long silence, wanted to talk about Shannon.

'Thanks for letting me come,' he said quietly. 'I guess it wasn't as relaxed a day for you as usual.'

'I was a bit on tenterhooks,' she admitted. She didn't tell him that already Callie had guessed he was Shannon's father.

He glanced at her, then said abruptly, with a trace of anger, 'You can't keep Shannon hidden away forever, Lee. Soon she's going to start asking more questions, she'll want to know more about you and your life. She's already suffering from an identity crisis. She knows the Morrises are not her real family, but you're a bit of an enigma. When we were out in the stables grooming and stabling the horses before tea tonight, she asked me if I thought you'd be angry if she asked if she could live with you.'

'Angry?' Lee was stunned. 'She's never. . .'

Trent said gently, 'She may be wondering why you've never suggested it. She's at the age to wonder, Lee. She may even feel you don't want her, that you've rejected her.'

Lee was wounded. 'How could she think that? I go evey weekend to see her. I spend as much time as I can with her.' It hurt a little that Trent had only to appear on the scene and Shannon was showering him with confidences.

'You could have her to live with you now,' Trent urged, and when she protested, he went on firmly, 'People in Shearwater would soon get used to the idea. She's already got it worked out. She'll have to change schools at the end of the year, and she asked me to find out whether you'd consider having her to live with you then. There's a suitable high school in Shearwater, I gather.'

Lee clasped her head in her hands. 'She said all this to you?'

'Maybe I was easier to talk to, being a stranger.' He gave her a wry sideways look. 'Fathers and daughters do sometimes have a special rapport.' There was a note of pride in his voice that Lee couldn't ignore.

But she felt as though she had neglected Shannon in some way. 'And you promised to talk to me about it?'

'How could I not?'

The thought of Shannon wanting to live with her made Lee feel a rush of affection. Her daughter actually wanted to live with her, and was afraid she might not be welcome. Oh, Shannon, she thought, if you only knew how much I want it too.

'She asked me something else,' Trent went on, amusement colouring his voice.

'What?' Lee was almost fearful now.

There was a deep silence as he expertly manoeuvred the car around a double bend in the road, then he said, deadpan, 'She asked me if my intentions were honourable.'

Lee almost choked. 'She asked you what?'

'If I was going to marry you.'

She was mortified. 'What did you say?'

'I said we hadn't talked about it yet.' He slid a sidelong glance at her. 'She seemed rather disappointed.'

'Trent, you don't really want to marry me,' Lee was almost relieved that the subject had finally come up again.

'We have quite a lot in common,' he pointed out, with a not altogether tongue-in-cheek smile. 'Medicine, jazz—our daughter. We're even rather attracted to each other. . .'

Lee made a strangled sound in her throat. He darted a swift glance in her direction again, saying rather harshly, 'Lee, your daughter needs a father. Do you think you should deprive her when her real father is willing?'

She swallowed on a tight larynx. It was almost emotional blackmail. She could not answer him.

When they arrived at the garage, Trent drew up in the forecourt, but did not switch off the car engine.

'Thanks for coming to my rescue today,' said Lee.

He reached across and ruffled her hair. 'I enjoyed it.'

His face was shadowed, but his features were strongly outlined in the lights from the motel and the street, and she was painfully reminded of a younger face, in the moonlight, making her stomach churn in precisely the same erotic way.

'See you tomorrow.' She slid out of the car, slammed the door and gave him a casual wave. She was too far away for him to see the tears in her eyes.

CHAPTER SIX

'Good weekend?' asked Zena, as she breezed into Lee's office next morning. She had a speculative look in her eye which put Lee on her guard immediately.

'Yes, thanks,' she answered automatically. 'Did you?'

'Great,' said Zena. She placed her palms flat on the desktop and leaned towards Lee. 'A little bird saw you getting into Dr Allingham's car on Sunday morning.'

It was so unexpected that Lee went deep pink. She could not deny it. 'My bike broke down,' she said. 'Luckily he happened to see me wheeling it back to the garage, and offered me a lift. I was going to lunch with friends.'

Zena looked dubious as well as disappointed. 'Lucky you anyway,' she said rather drily.

Lee forced a smile and said in a firm tone, 'Don't start making mountains out of molehills, Zena. There's quite enough gossip around this hospital already.'

'None about you, though,' said Zena with a grin.

'And neither should there be,' Lee retorted.

Zena perched for a moment on the corner of the desk regarding her thoughtfully. 'No, you're not the kind of person people gossip about—you wouldn't give them cause. I hope Michael Farrow appreciates that. Are you going to marry him, Lee?'

Lee stood up. 'What I'm going to do, Zena, is check on our patients, and I'm sure you've got plenty to do too.'

Zena took the rebuff good-naturedly and went out. Lee, as she always did as soon as she came on in the morning, did her round of the patients. There were two she particularly wanted to see that morning.

'Hello, Sharon,' she greeted the patient whose post-operative condition had precipitated a crisis and a strong reprimand from Trent. 'How are you today?'

'Good morning, Sister,' Sharon Price said brightly, but with a certain wistfulness. 'I feel fine. How much longer am I going to be here?'

Lee unhooked her chart from the end of the bed and studied it. She was pleased to see that all the weekend observations were normal. 'This looks fine,' she said. 'Maybe Dr Allingham will let you go home in a day or two.' Trent had been adamant that she should not be discharged too soon.

'He's nice, isn't he?' said Sharon, rolling her eyes a little. 'I was really scared until he came along and took charge. He sort of makes you think everything's going to be all right, doesn't he?'

Lee smiled. 'He's a very competent doctor. We're lucky to have him.'

She continued on her round, stopping for a few words with each of the gynae patients and also the new mothers. There were few serious problems, everyone was getting better or had had a trouble-free delivery, and the atmosphere in the wards was one of optimism and even gaiety. But there was one private room where Lee knew that the outlook was still not so bright.

Deliberately, she left until last visiting Rachel Armstrong. The girl was sitting in a chair, reading a paperback novel. She looked up, unsmiling, as Lee came in, and answered her greeting with only her usual perfunctory grunt. She was still pale and her dark hair needed combing. Her pregnancy was very advanced.

Lee said cheerfully, 'I half expected to find you with a bouncing boy or girl this morning.'

Rachel grimaced. 'I wish it'd hurry up. I hate being here. I want to get it over with.'

Lee drew up a chair. 'Do you still want to keep the baby?'

'Of course I do. You don't go through all this just to hand it over to someone else, do you?' She spoke with bravado, then she looked at Lee and her face crumpled and tears started falling. 'Why can't they believe me? They keep on and on at me to have it adopted. I suppose I'll have to in the end. How can I bring up a baby on my own? They won't help me. . .' She scowled. 'I suppose you've come to try and talk some sense into me, like my mother asked you to.'

Lee gently took hold of her hand. 'No, Rachel, I haven't. You're the one who has to make the decision about whether you keep your baby or not.'

Rachel looked astonished. 'I thought you'd be on their side!'

'I'm not on anyone's "side". But I do think that if you want to keep your baby you should be allowed to, so long as you realise what a huge responsibility it will be.' Lee smiled hopefully. 'And you never know, your parents might change their attitude once they see your baby.'

'They wish it would be born dead,' said Rachel harshly. 'Sometimes, so do I. That would solve everything, wouldn't it?' She wiped her tears away and sniffed, fumbling for a handkerchief in the pocket of her gown. 'What would you do, Sister? If you were me, would you keep your baby or give it up for adoption?'

Lee did not hesitate. 'I wouldn't give my baby up for adoption,' she said. 'And no one has the right to insist that you do.'

Rachel's mouth firmed in determination. She suddenly reached out and clasped Lee's hand. 'Help me . . .tell me what to do. . .tell me how I can do it. Please. . . I'm so frightened, Sister. I want my baby, but I'm scared I won't be able to look after it properly.'

Lee soothed her gently and talked as reassuringly as she knew how for some minutes. She wished she could tell her about her own experiences, but she couldn't. However, her earlier misgivings began to fade as Rachel responded to what she was saying, and when Lee's pager finally cut short their conversation she felt more confident that Rachel would cope. All she needed was the reassurance that what she wanted to do was right.

'If you want to talk about it again,' Lee urged as she was leaving, 'just call me.'

Rachel was almost cheerful as she said, 'Thanks. Thanks a lot.'

As Lee left her room, she almost collided with Trent. After yesterday, she felt uncomfortable looking at him.

'How's Rachel?' he asked.

'Fine. We had a chat. I don't know if I did the right thing, and I still think it was a bit unethical, but I encouraged her to keep the baby.' She moved away from him, patting her pager. 'I was just paged. I'd better see who wants me.'

'I do,' he said.

Lee felt warm colour flood into her cheeks. She wished he wouldn't look at her like that. 'What do you want?' she asked.

He cast caution to the winds. 'I want you to marry me.'

'Trent, we can't talk about it now,' she said desperately.

'When?'

She swallowed hard. 'There's nothing to talk about. I can't marry you, that's all.'

The following weekend Shannon was staying with friends, so Lee did not go to the farm on Sunday. She took the opportunity to have a relaxing day at the beach, choosing a secluded cove she knew where there was unlikely to be anyone else. A quiet laze on the beach, she told herself, was just what she needed to ease the tensions that had been building up in her over the last few weeks.

Not being a true redhead, she tanned easily, but she was not one to ignore the warnings about UV and skin cancer. She had seen too often the ravages of too much sunlight on skin that was never meant to be exposed with such ritual dedication as it was in Australia. After applying lashings of sun-screen after her shower, she slipped into a one-piece green swimsuit, topped it with a floral beach coat and large shady hat, packed the sandwiches she had prepared earlier and a cooler of orange juice, and set off for Wreckers' Cove, a tiny inlet which few people knew about and where she could be assured of privacy. That it was situated right below the cliffs beyond which lay Hilsborough was unimportant, since no one could see the cove from the house, or even from the clifftops, because of the overhang. It was accessible only over rocks from the beach, so she walked.

In the sheltered pool that was enclosed by rocky

outcrops, and where the surf broke long before it reached the pool, Lee swam lazily, enjoying the cool satiny touch of the water, and the caress of a light breeze. It was a perfect day, not too hot, not too cold, and she felt her taut muscles gradually relax.

In a sudden mad moment of euphoria, because she was quite alone in the cove and likely to remain so, she threw off her swimsuit and tossed it up on to the beach. She luxuriated naked in the water, wondering why anyone ever bothered to wear a costume. When, after making sure there was still no one around, she floated in to shore and stepped gingerly to where she had thrown her bathing suit, she decided to enjoy her freedom for a little longer, so did not put it back on.

She ran back to the shady spot under the rocks where she had left her clothes. If anyone appeared she would spot them in time to slip on her beach coat before they saw her. She opened her lunch packet and poured out a plastic cup of orange juice. Having eaten, she covered herself in sun-screen once more and moved into the sun, lying flat on her back on her towel to sunbathe. Ten minutes each side was all she would allow herself, just enough to even up her tan, not long enough to cause any damage to her skin.

She didn't intend to fall asleep, but the exertions of the week had caught up with her and, relaxed after her swim and lunch, she closed her eyes and drifted off. She woke in the shade. But not of the rocks, as she quickly discovered when she raised her head a little. Sitting on the sand in precisely the place to cast a shadow the length of her was Trent Allingham, in brief black bathing trunks and a white canvas hat.

After freezing in horror for a moment, Lee flung on her beach coat and clutched it tightly around her. 'What are you doing here?' she demanded as though he were a Peeping Tom.

Trent smiled amiably. 'You looked so peaceful I didn't want to disturb you even to cover you with your beach coat. You looked like someone who deserved to rest. But I was a bit worried about how long you might have been in the sun, so I organised a shadow.'

Lee was angry, embarrassed and amused all together. 'How long have you been here?' she demanded.

'Long enough to get cramp in my legs,' he said, massaging an ankle. 'But the view was worth it!' He looked amused at her frantic haste to cover up.

'Nobody ever comes here,' she said, attempting to excuse her nudity.

'I do. It's only a short climb down the cliffs.' He jerked a hand upwards.

'You can't climb down, it's too steep,' she insisted.

He shook his head. 'Oh, yes, you can, if you know a way. I did it often as a boy. There used to be a sea eagle's nest on top of those rocks.' He pointed to an inaccessible crag.

'I hope you weren't stealing eggs,' Lee said.

'No. Even if I'd wanted to I couldn't have got close enough. But I wasn't interested in stealing eggs, only in watching them hatch.'

'Early interest in obstetrics coming to the fore,' she suggested, smiling. Her outrage at his intrusion on her privacy was subsiding.

'I suppose so. The birth of new lives, the reproductive cycle, has always fascinated me.' He glanced at her cooler. 'You couldn't spare me a drink, I suppose?'

'Of course. There's plenty.' Lee poured some orange juice into the plastic cup. 'Sorry, there's only one cup.'

He took it from her. 'Is that a warning to use my left

hand?' he laughed. 'Ever heard the one about the doctor who visited the old lady who was none too clean in her habits? He accepted a cup of tea and decided he'd better drink from the left-hand side. As he gulped the tea down, she said, "Oh, doctor, what a coincidence, you're left-handed too!"'

Lee laughed. 'I thought that story was about a vicar.'

He grinned at her, then said seriously, 'Are you aware that you seem to have had a good effect on the Armstrongs? I hear Rachel's sticking to her guns about keeping the baby, and her parents are showing signs of softening their attitude.'

Rachel's baby had been born on Thursday, a lightweight but perfectly healthy infant, and when they arrived to visit their daughter Lee had found herself practically lecturing Rachel's parents. To her amazement they had taken it meekly, and the atmosphere in Rachel's room had greatly improved.

'I'm sure Rachel will make a good mother,' Lee said.

'Like you. . .'

'I'm not a good mother,' Lee denied. 'It's Callie who's brought Shannon up. I'm just a weekend mother.'

'Shannon thinks the sun shines out of you, though,' Trent told her.

He finished the orange juice and put the cup back on top of the cooler. He stretched out so that his head was near her knees, which she had half drawn under her. He ran his fingers slowly across her calf and knee.

'Nice legs, Lee.'

She tried to distance herself a little. 'I'll have varicose veins by the time I'm forty,' she joked. 'Occupational hazard.' She wished he wasn't so close. Bare-chested, he was even more disturbing, and her heart was already racing.

'Why don't you go for a swim?' she said. 'You don't have to be my beach umbrella now!'

'If you come too.' His eyes were teasing. 'Either you can put your swimsuit back on, or I'll take mine off.'

Lee blushed. No way was she going skinny-dipping with Trent Allingham. 'It's time I went home.' She made a move, but he grasped her ankle and she fell back on the towel, clutching the beach coat around her.

'Not yet, Lee,' he said softly. 'Not yet. . .' His hand slid smoothly from her ankle up her leg and a warm palm caressed her thigh, then strayed further up under her beach coat to her waist, until he cupped her breast in his fingers and teased her nipple.

'Stop it, Trent!' Lee protested, but he took no notice, and she seemed unable to match her words with action. His mouth was too soon capturing hers, cajoling her trembling lips into responses that had hitherto existed only in memory—the memory of a moonlit night, with the rhythm of the sea in the background, and the darkness of the old summerhouse at Hilsborough hiding their ecstasy.

'You're beautiful, Lee,' he murmured huskily now, as then. His mouth moved on hers with increasing pressure and his tongue met with hers in the kind of erotic conversation lovers invented. He broke away briefly to look into her eyes. Lee felt her muscles melting, and the warm tingling sensations of need stirring her whole body.

But if she let Trent make love to her now, and there was no doubt that he wanted to, she might find herself in as lamentable a situation as she had years ago. Trent was hurriedly undoing the belt on her beach coat. He flung the wrap open and lowered his body on to hers. A long sigh escaped him as he brought his mouth to her breasts and tangled his fingers in her hair. His leg pressed hard between her thighs, exciting an involuntary gasp from her.

After a moment he raised his head and smiled at her. 'I hate your hair this colour and short, but the rest of you is delicious. Lee. . .' The question was in his eyes, the pleading, the urgent need that finding her naked on the beach had aroused.

Pinned beneath him, Lee was conscious that it was not just his weight keeping her there, but her own treacherous needs which his warm skin and caressing hands were rapidly awakening. She wanted desperately to make love to him because she was *in love* with this man.

Trent ran a finger in small circles around her earlobes, dropping kisses on her mouth and subtly moving himself against her to hasten her compliance. Lee closed her eyes. It was so hard not to. . .

It was Trent who brought back reality. 'I guess we'd better be sensible.' He smiled. 'I didn't come down for a swim prepared to be seduced, did you?'

'No!' Lee, ashamed of her weakness for him, turned her back and pulled on her swimsuit, which was now dry, bunching the beach coat around her again and tightly tying the belt. When she faced him again, he was still watching her, leaning on his elbows.

'Lee. . .' he said, half teasing, 'marry me, and then we can make love all the time.'

'I'm going,' she said firmly. 'And I suggest you have that swim to cool you down.' She smiled at him because she wasn't really angry. 'See you tomorrow.'

He stood up. 'Yeah. Bryce and I and some of the

other medical staff are having a meeting to discuss the opening of the new wing. I'd like you to come along. There are still a few loose ends to tie that concern your staff.'

'Of course.'

'It'll be a major task moving everything first, and we want to be quite ready when the day comes. Your organising skills will be a great help.'

'What time's the meeting?' Lee asked, glad to have the conversation back to ordinary topics.

'Ten. OK?'

'Fine. See you then.'

She picked up her belongings and, with a brief goodbye, set off across the beach to the rocks, which she would pick her way across until she reached the main bathing beach.

Suddenly tears stung her eyes and she had difficulty curbing the almost overwhelming desire to turn round, even to run back into Trent's arms. She stumbled on a protruding rock and lost her balance, falling heavily. A jagged rock scraped down her thigh, making her gasp with pain. She stared at the droplets of blood that sprang up all over the graze and fumbled in her beach bag for a tissue.

'Damn!' she whimpered. 'Ouch!' There was sand in the wound and it was already starting to sting. She buried her head in her hands, unable to get up yet.

The swish of running steps on the sand made her turn her head. Trent had evidently been watching her before going for his swim. 'I saw you trip,' he said with concern as he dropped to his haunches. 'Have you hurt yourself?'

Lee pulled a face and showed him her thigh. 'It's OK. Just a graze.'

He examined it closely. 'You've got more than a graze. There's a deep cut at one end. Come on, I'll take you up to the house and dress it for you.'

Her skin was tingling at his touch. She said, 'There's no need. I'm a nurse, remember? I can do it myself.'

'It's a bit of an awkward spot,' he said, 'and quite nasty. I think you should have an antibiotic. I can give you that—you can't.'

Lee was surprised at how shaky she felt. She let Trent take her arm and guide her back up the narrow beach to the foot of the cliff. It suddenly looked an impossible climb. 'I—I can't,' she murmured. 'I'd better go the other way, Trent, it's flat. I'll see Dr Ransome in the morning and he can give me a shot if he thinks it's necessary.' She made to retrace her steps, but Trent was not having it.

'You're coming with me.' And before she could protest, he had scooped her up in his arms and was carrying her up the cliff path.

Lee, clinging on to her bag and cooler, felt a fool, but also relieved. Whether it was the sun, Trent himself, or the shock of falling and hurting herself, she didn't know, but she felt quite dizzy. She laid her head against his warm shoulder and felt infinitely grateful for his insistence.

It was not as far up the cliff as it seemed, and Trent managed the climb, even with his burden, in only a few minutes. In a few more he was carrying her into the house, to a small sitting-room off the hallway, where he insisted she stretch out on a chaise longue. Lee carefully arranged her beach coat so that blood would not seep on to the upholstery.

'I'll have you fixed up in no time,' he promised.

'Won't be long.' He looked back as he reached the door. 'I expect you'd like a cup of tea. I'll tell Edna.'

Lee was hardly surprised to find Trent's ministrations to be gentle and thorough. After all, this wasn't the first time he had looked after her, and she'd had plenty of opportunity to observe his expertise and bedside manner at the hospital.

He exercised great care in cleansing the graze, removing all the sand, even picking out elusive grains with tweezers. Lee found the intimacy of his touch on her thigh almost unbearable, but now he seemed concerned only for her welfare and gave no hint of his former ardour.

'That should do,' he said at last, having applied a light dressing. 'Try not to get it too wet for a day or two until the scab forms.' He gave her a shot of erythromycin in case of infection, saying, 'You'd better let Dr Ransome take a look at it tomorrow.' Suddenly his eyes twinkled. 'Be careful, though. It's a mighty attractive thigh!'

Lee's tension dissolved. 'Trent. . .really!' She rose gingerly, wincing. 'I must go home.'

He pushed her gently back. 'You haven't had your tea yet.' As he spoke Edna came in with a tray. She fussed a little over Lee's injury, then left them. Trent poured and offered Lee cake. He sprawled in a chair near hers and for a while seemed to have nothing more on his mind than afternoon tea. Finally he said, 'Where did you leave your bike?'

'I didn't. I walked along the beach.'

He nodded. 'I'll drive you home.'

She was standing at the foot of the veranda steps, waiting for Trent to bring the car round, when she noticed a vehicle coming up the driveway. She recognised it at once; it was Francine Kennedy's car. The interior decorator arrived just as Trent drew up and leaned across to throw open the passenger door for Lee. He got out to greet Francine, who flung her arms around his neck, kissed him and said,

'Hello, darling! I can stay three days this time, isn't that wonderful?'

She saw Lee and said hello. Lee looked at her smart white suit and red silk shirt, her beautifully manicured hands and make-up, and received, although she didn't need it, a forceful reminder that she and Trent belonged in different worlds, that he and Francine were probably lovers, and that marrying Trent was the last thing she ever ought to think of doing, even for Shannon's sake.

CHAPTER SEVEN

'I HONESTLY don't know how we'll ever manage it,' Zena moaned a few days later after a staff meeting to discuss the transfer to the new building. 'How are we going to shift everyone *and* cope with nursing them? I bet we have every known emergency.'

'We very well may if you keep willing disaster to strike.' Lee laughed at her colleague. 'Cheer up, Zena, it'll soon be over. Don't forget that at the official opening you'll be shaking the hand of the mayor and chatting up the visiting medicos for all you're worth, and loving every minute.'

'That I doubt,' said Zena, putting instruments into the autoclave for sterilising. She added, 'Trent Allingham might be worth chatting up, though.' She gave Lee a sly look.

'I thought you were keen on Andrew?'

Zena snorted. 'You'd need the hide of a rhinoceros and the patience of a saint to get involved with that man. You'd spend three-quarters of your life watching in fear and trembling while he fell out of the sky on the end of a parachute, disappeared under the ocean or tried to break his neck dangling from a kite! Stress is what I don't need any more of.'

'Hang-gliders are a bit more advanced than kites,' Lee said, amused at Zena's vehemence. The romance obviously had some powerful obstacles.

Zena was not to be pacified. 'And what's more, he'd

be more likely to notice that a piece of equipment was missing than if I was!'

'Well, never mind. We're getting a new junior registrar. He might be just your cup of tea.'

'As Dr Allingham is yours?'

Lee pretended to be looking for something in one of the cupboards. 'Hardly. Anyway, he likes sophisticated ladies.' She grabbed a packet of spatulas and escaped, too quickly to hear Zena mutter,

'So who are you kidding, Sister Dennison?'

A few minutes later Trent came to Lee's office. 'You have some new maternity admissions for me to meet?' He always made a special point of seeing every new patient before her baby was born, or she underwent surgery.

Lee got up, reaching for a sheaf of papers. 'Now?'

'If that's all right? It's not ward drill time, is it?'

She smiled at the joking reference to the aerobics class which she had instituted as part of the antenatal care for mothers admitted for one reason or another some time before their babies were due.

'No. And there are only two new patients. Mrs Wendy Benson, whose admission was arranged by Dr Lamb because she's expecting triplets, and Mrs Pauline Irwin who's diabetic.' She added, 'Do you want to see the gynae cases too? Two D & Cs and a fistula, that's all.'

'Mmm,' he murmured, skimming the admission cards as she handed them to him.

Lee went on, 'We've quite a few maternity beds booked for this week. We could be extra busy if the babes are all on schedule.'

Trent nodded, and looked up at her. 'I suppose you'll be glad when the move's over?'

'Everyone will be! Zena's been having nightmares for weeks!'

He laughed. 'She would! I know it's going to be a big disruption, but with careful planning we should be able to manage the change-over smoothly. This area will continue to function in conjunction with the new department for a while. It'll have to, otherwise we might have a problem coping with emergencies.'

'Which will mean a lot of dashing back and forth for staff,' Lee commented. She gave a pointed smile. 'No doubt you'd say, good for our figures, to be run off our feet!'

Trent took the remark as a cue. 'How's your thigh?'

Lee paused, her hand on the door-handle. 'Just a bit itchy now. It's practically healed.'

'I thought I saw you limping.'

For a moment she thought he was going to demand to see the injury, or lift her uniform skirt himself to inspect it, but he didn't. 'I did a bit at first,' she admitted. 'The skin pulled a lot and was quite painful, more so than you'd expect with just a graze.'

'You tore quite a large area of skin,' he reminded her. 'And it went quite deep in places. The skin on the inside of your thigh is very sensitive.'

And how! Lee thought with a rise in blood heat, as she remembered how his touch had sent shock waves to all parts of her.

They entered the small three-bed ward where Pauline Irwin was sitting up in an armchair. Lee asked her to lie on the bed, and drew the curtains around it.

Trent was not conducting a general examination, so no gloves or instruments were needed. His stethoscope was all he wanted for this preliminary introduction to the patient. He whipped it out of his pocket and slung it around his neck.

Mrs Irwin was clearly nervous. She had only recently moved to the town when her husband had been transferred in his job.

While he positioned the stethoscope to listen to the foetal heartbeat, Trent reassured her. 'Your doctor in Melbourne sent all your particulars, Pauline. You've been admitted to hospital three times for insulin stabilisation during your pregnancy; is that right?'

The young woman nodded. Lee saw the anxiety in her eyes and felt a wave of sympathy.

Pauline Irwin said in an almost inaudible voice, 'Jerry said we shouldn't have children, and we didn't intend to. . . He said the risks. . .'

Trent patted her hand. 'Now listen to me, young lady. You're not the first and I dare say you won't be the last diabetes mellitus sufferer to have a baby. It's true there are risks attached, and I'm not minimising them, but so long as we keep an eye on you, there's no reason why you shouldn't have a perfectly healthy baby just like anyone else. Your doctor in Melbourne has rightly watched your metabolism very closely, and although going in and out of hospital has doubtless been tedious it's what will ensure that you give birth without too many problems.'

'He told me I'd have to have a Caesarean delivery,' the patient said, her disappointment plain.

Trent was non-committal. 'We'll see about that. If you and the baby keep going along all right, as you now are, it might not be necessary.'

'Isn't there a risk the baby might die?' Pauline asked.

He nodded. 'A greater risk in the later stages than in a normal pregnancy, but don't worry, if we think there's any real risk, we'll do what's necessary. Meanwhile, you just relax and look forward to a normal, natural birth.'

Pauline had one more question. 'My doctor in Melbourne said there was a fifty-fifty chance the baby will be diabetic too.' She pursed her lips. 'My father was diabetic, and I inherited it.'

Trent raised an eyebrow. 'And is it a big problem?'

'Only when you want to have babies!'

'But you're glad you were born?'

Pauline laughed. 'Of course I am, but. . .'

'Now don't you go blaming yourself if your baby does turn out to have the inherited gene. Just remember that you've got all the experience to help him or her cope. And remember too that there's a bit better than an even chance your baby won't be diabetic. So stop worrying!'

Outside the ward Lee said, in some surprise, 'You mean you might not do a Caesar?'

'We'll see—as I told her, and I meant it.' As Lee opened her mouth to say something, he interrupted, 'Yes, I know most obstetricians are keen on Caesarean section in these cases because of the high risk of intrauterine death in the last few weeks, but I'm not one of them. Careful monitoring of the patient and baby can obviate those risks. I think all women should enjoy natural vaginal birth if at all possible.' He paused. 'Wouldn't you agree that it's an experience not to be missed?'

Lee gave a faint smile. 'I had a difficult pregnancy and a protracted labour. . .' She looked up at him. 'But yes. . .yes, it is.' Momentarily she relived the moment when it was finally all over, when she had held Shannon's tiny body in her arms for the first time, and experienced the pure joy of motherhood.

'And that if possible fathers should be present at the birth?'

'Yes, definitely.' Looking at Trent now, at Shannon's father, Lee deeply regretted that he had not been there at the time to share it with her, and felt some guilt for having deprived him of the experience. It was almost as though he was blaming her for not telling him. 'Shall we see Mrs Benson next?' she said in a cool voice. 'What reassuring words, I wonder, can you find to say to a prospective mother of triplets?'

Trent, with a wicked gleam in his eyes, laughed. 'Don't do it again!'

Three weeks later, the transfer of the maternity and gynaecological functions to the new wing was carried out with the minimum of disruption. Preparations gathered momentum all week until on the Friday the final move was made. Lee, working longer hours than her usual shifts, had little time to reflect on her private problems; there was too much to do at the hospital, and at night she was so dead tired that she slept instantly.

Trent was as good an organiser as he was a doctor, Lee had discovered. Bryce hovered around, but seemed content to let Trent handle things. He had planned the day like a military manoeuvre, with everyone allocated tasks and times to do them. His aim, he told Lee, was to smooth the transition so that in the event of an emergency they were not caught between two stools.

Which turned out to be wise. Lee was packing paperwork in boxes when she heard an ambulance, siren blaring, come into the forecourt just below her office window. She heard ambulances arriving all the time, so paid little heed to it. But within minutes her phone was ringing. Casualty wanted Dr Allingham and he wasn't answering his beeper.

'He's probably in the new wing,' Lee told them.

'The phones aren't connected there yet,' came the reply.

'I know. Telecom's supposed to be here this morning.' Lee asked, 'What's the problem?'

'Woman in labour. She's had a fall and the baby's showing signs of stress. It's not due for four weeks.'

Lee hesitated only a second. 'I'll see if I can find him.'

As she dashed out of her office, Zena appeared carrying a large cardboard box marked in felt pen in large letters 'disposable bedpans'.

'I'm just taking these over,' she said. 'They got left behind when the rest of the stuff went.'

'Leave that,' Lee said briskly. 'We've got an emergency. A woman's had a fall that's brought on early labour. Have you seen Trent?'

'He's in the new wing,' Zena confirmed.

'But he's not answering his pager,' said Lee. 'Look, get the delivery-room ready—wc haven't moved the gear from there yet. And the incubator.'

Leaving Zena to cope, Lee flew across the connecting bridge to the new wing. She found Trent in the new theatre suite, advising on the installation of lighting. Breathlessly she told him about the emergency.

'They've been trying to call you on the beeper,' she said. 'Is there something wrong with it?'

Trent shoved a hand in his coat pocket, then frowned. 'I must have left it in my office. Isn't that always the way? I'm not usually forgetful.' He seemed angry with himself as, coat tails flapping, he strode back with Lee, who had to run to keep up. 'You'd better get hold of Dr Norton,' he said, as they marched along the corridor towards the delivery-room. 'If we've got a prem we'll need her.'

Lee left him to scrub while she contacted the hospital's peadiatrician who would direct the nursing care of the premature baby. Having done that, she sped to give Trent whatever assistance was needed.

The emergency was over quite quickly. The patient, a young woman in her twenties, was delivered of a baby boy who was placed immediately in the humidicrib. Neither the mother or the baby had been seriously injured in the fall, but the mother had sustained some bruising to her forehead and arms and was shocked. She had tried to protect her unborn child as she toppled off a small pair of steps while changing a lightbulb.

'We've got those old-fashioned high ceilings,' she told Lee later. 'I shouldn't have tried to change the bulb, I should have waited till my husband came home, but I wanted to finish painting the nursery and it was a bit dreary in there today.' She looked fearful. 'He'll be all right, won't he?'

'Of course,' said Lee. 'He'll have to stay here for a few weeks, but as he's got no physical disabilities I expect you'll be taking him home quite soon.'

To Lee's and everyone else's relief that was the only crisis of the day, and by the end of Lee's shift the move was almost complete. She stayed to supervise the transfer of the last of the patients, then checked her office in case she had left anything behind. The old department was to be gutted, she'd been told, and used to extend the men's and women's surgical wards, as well as to set up a separate oncology ward.

Trent found her closing the office door. 'Well, that's more or less it, Lee.'

'Thank goodness,' she said wearily. 'It's been quite a day. Quite a week, in fact.' She added, 'But it could have been worse, I suppose!' and laughed ironically.

Trent caught her shoulders. 'But not much better. You did a great job, Lee. All your staff did, but thanks to your efficiency.'

His praise gave her a lift. 'I hope I'll remember where to go on Monday morning!'

He looked at her intently for a moment, then said in a rush, 'You'll be seeing Shannon this weekend?'

Lee nodded.

'Anything special planned?'

'No. We'll probably go riding, swimming, as usual.' She half held her breath, wondering if he was going to ask if he could come too. He had not mentioned marriage again since that day at the cove, and Lee believed that the novelty of discovering he was a father was probably beginning to wear off. No doubt the fact that Francine had been staying at Hilsborough again—Lee had encountered her once in the town—had something to do with it.

Trent seemed to hesitate, then he said, 'There are a lot of places along the coast I haven't been to for years. I thought I'd do a little exploring. Company would be nice. How about a picnic?'

Lee didn't know how to turn him down. Loving him made her want to be near him even if it would ultimately make the hurt worse.

'All right. Shannon will enjoy that.'

'She's a great kid.' He pulled a wry face. 'I suppose I'm not supposed to say that!'

* * *

The opening of the new Wilma Brownlow wing, named for the first matron of Shearwater Community Hospital, went without a hitch. The mayor cut the ribbon, staff and patients cheered, and champagne flowed.

Lee, in uniform specially for the occasion even though it was Saturday and she was officially off duty, found herself giving quotes to the Press and smiling for photographers with patients and staff in the new wards. She was even photographed once with Trent with his arm paternally around her shoulders.

Many ex-patients were there, including of course a lot of children and babies. Lee was surprised and delighted to see Rachel and her baby, together with her parents. They had come down specially for the occasion. Rachel confided out of earshot of her parents, 'They love Paul—it's great. Thanks a lot for what you did.'

'I didn't. . .' Lee protested.

'You helped,' said Rachel simply. 'You gave me the confidence I needed to go through with it.' She added, 'I never wanted to be a lawyer like Dad. I'm going to be a teacher. They're disappointed, but they're resigned to it now.'

Lee just managed to whisper, 'Bravo!' before Rachel's parents joined them.

After the opening, in the evening, there was a staff dinner in the hospital dining-room. Bryce Summerlad gave another speech and personally thanked everyone who had contributed to the smooth change-over. There was laughter at the 'in' jokes, and more champagne ensured that the occasion was convivial. Zena, Lee noticed with a pang of envy, seemed to be getting on very well indeed with Andrew Collins. Her senior staff nurse and the young doctor looked decidedly intimate, their heads close together every time she caught a glimpse of them.

Trent followed Lee when she left. In the car park, he caught up with her and grasped her arm. 'Hang on a minute. . .'

She turned too quickly, which made her stagger; the champagne had made her a little light-headed. 'What's the matter?' she asked.

'You can't ride your motorbike like that,' Trent told her firmly.

Lee, her mind a little fuzzy, thought he must be referring to her clothes. She looked down at her jeans. 'But I've changed. . .'

'You've had too much champagne,' he said. 'Come on, I'll drive you. We'll fetch the bike tomorrow.'

'We're going on a picnic tomorrow,' she remembered. She swayed towards him. Trent caught her and propelled her towards his car. He shoved her in the passenger-seat and fastened the seatbelt across her slim figure. His hands brushing her breasts sent shivers along her spine.

She pretended to be indignant. 'You had champagne too,' she said as he got in beside her. 'You shouldn't drive. . .'

'I had one glass. The rest was mineral water.'

She pulled a face. 'I wish I'd thought of that. I'm afraid it has gone to my head a bit.'

'Champagne's like that,' he said as they left the hospital car park. 'It seems so innocuous you go on drinking it until suddenly it knocks you over.'

Lee felt an irrational resentment welling up in her. 'Yes—well, I suppose you know all about champagne. In the circles you move in, they don't drink much else.'

He chuckled softly. 'Oh, they knock back the hard stuff too, and the vintage wines.'

'I'm sure.' Lee's head fell back against the rest and in one second she was asleep.

She woke with a jolt to find Trent carrying her to her front door. 'Hey, put me down,' she protested, struggling, but he did not let her go until they reached the porch.

'You need a black coffee,' he said. 'Ask me in and I'll make one for both of us.'

Lee hesitated. Trent in her ordinary little house was not something she had ever envisaged. But he'd been good enough to see her home. She slid her key in the door and turned it. She was sobering up quickly now. 'Come in. I'll make it.'

She installed him in the living-room while she made the coffee. To Lee, coming back with a tray, the room seemed even shabbier than the rooms at Hilsborough had looked. She switched off the central light and turned on the reading lamp. It made the atmosphere more intimate than she had intended.

They chatted about the events of the day, the success of the opening, the publicity it might have generated.

When Lee yawned, Trent said, 'I'm keeping you up.'

'I'm afraid I have to agree with that! I'll be falling asleep any minute. I don't mean to be rude, but. . .'

'What time tomorrow?' he asked.

She looked at him with longing and said, 'It's been a tiring day for you too. You don't have to. . .'

He said softly, 'I know I don't have to. I want to.' He fingered a strand of her hair, twisting it idly, sending shivers down her spine again. 'We both need to relax.'

'Eight-thirty?' she suggested in a wavering voice. 'I'll make a picnic lunch.'

He shook his head. 'No need—Edna's volunteered.

She was always good at picnics, and jumped at the chance.'

Lee was anxious. 'You told her about Shannon and me?'

'I've told no one about Shannon and you,' he assured her. 'I told her I was taking two friends on a picnic, that's all.'

She stood up and he rose too. He caught hold of her hands and raised them to his lips. 'Goodnight, Lee.'

'Goodnight, Trent, and thanks. . .' She lifted her face to his as she spoke, and he swiftly caught it between spread palms, tilting her chin and placing his lips on hers.

He kissed her with unexpected tenderness, then drew her into his arms and let passion take over. Lee's heart surged with love and desire and she was in no state to put up resistance. All she wanted was for Trent to kiss her until they were both breathless, and he was only too happy to oblige.

Eventually he raised his head and smiled into her eyes. 'I'd better go. If I stay a minute longer I shall have to make love to you.'

The word hovered on Lee's lips. *Stay*, her heart whispered, *stay with me and love me*, but through the haze of longing that almost overwhelmed her cold reason showed its face. A brief affair with Trent Allingham was not what she wanted, and what she did want—for Trent to want to marry her because he loved her—was more unattainable than the moon.

'See you tomorrow,' she said, moving toward the door. 'Thanks again for bringing me home.'

'My pleasure.' He paused at the door and brushed her lips with his again, but her resolve was strong and she did not change her mind.

CHAPTER EIGHT

LEE woke with a headache and recollections she would have preferred not to have. Oh, why had Trent come back to Shearwater to mess up her life? She'd been drifting towards marrying Michael—providing he was prepared to accept Shannon, of course—but now Trent was turning her life upside down again.

She sighed as she let herself remember, and smiled. It was all very well to say she had been foolish to fall in love with Trent, but what could have prevented it? Love just happened, and for her it had begun to happen from the moment he'd said, 'I'll take you for a spin, if you like.' In his leathers and helmet he had cut a romantic figure, and she had climbed up behind him on the Harley-Davidson, her heart pounding with joy. She had fallen in love with him then because he was strong and kind and made her feel wonderful, and she'd fallen in love with him all over again now for precisely the same reasons.

Her father would have hit the roof if he'd known she was seeing him. He had thought she was too young at sixteen, even seventeen, to have boyfriends, and he certainly wouldn't have approved of her being with Trent. Not that Trent had really been a boyfriend, even though she'd seen him often over a whole year. It was her fault she'd fallen in love with him.

Suddenly realising what time it was, Lee scrambled out of bed and hurriedly got ready. It was just as well

Edna had offered to make the picnic lunch, she thought, because she would never have had time.

A loud tooting on the car's horn announced Trent's arrival. Lee grabbed her bag and squashed a hat on her head, then locked the door behind her. Trent was standing by the car, looking towards the motel. Lee swallowed, not sure which was stronger, the desire to run to him or away from him.

He turned to her. 'You look saucy in that hat.' He wanted to kiss her, but thought the better of it. She'd be worried someone might see. He opened the passenger door for her.

'How's the motel business?' he asked as they drove off. 'I noticed the sign said "No vacancies".'

'We're usually full,' Lee told him. 'It does good business. Dad made a wise move building on that spare land next to the garage. I regret to say, though, that I don't have much to do with the motel. Lana and Geoff are first-rate managers and I just leave them to it. Dad's accountant takes care of the financial side for the motel and the garage. I haven't got a head for figures anyway.' She laughed. 'There was a time, though, when I had to live on the smell of an oily rag and balance my budget—when I was doing my training in Melbourne and sending Callie keep for Shannon. She said she didn't want it, but she had kids of her own, so I couldn't sponge on her. Small farms like theirs don't make fortunes these days.' She stopped abruptly. Why was she rattling on like that?

Trent glanced at her. 'If you'd told me about Shannon I would have looked after you. The one big advantage I've always had is not being hard up.'

'Lucky for you, but I didn't want to be a skeleton in the Allinghams' cupboard,' Lee said rather tartly.

'You're so damned independent!'

'Am I? I always seem to be having to depend on someone. Callie. You. . .'

'You've hardly depended on me!'

Her voice softened. 'Oh, yes, I have. You took over when I collapsed after Dad died. I'll always be grateful for that, Trent.'

'The least anyone could do.' He sounded embarrassed.

A silence stretched for several miles, as though each had private thoughts to occupy them. Finally Lee broke it by mentioning work.

'I can't believe we're actually in the new wing at last. You did a fantastic job organising it, Trent. And the opening went like a dream.' She chuckled. 'Zena's really chuffed being promoted to charge sister on Gynae. I'll miss her, of course. She's a terrific nurse, she deserves promotion.'

They talked about the hospital for the rest of the way to the farm, where Shannon was impatiently waiting for them. She was delighted with the plan to have a picnic. All the way she chattered happily about school and her horse and the farm, and Lee tried not to think that this was how it might have been—lots of simple family outings—if things had been different, if Trent had not been who he was, and she who she was. . . We're still worlds apart, she reminded herself, and you'd better not forget that.

Like a sharp jab with a scalpel, Mrs Allingham's words came back vividly as they had often done in the long months of her pregnancy and again lately, the words that had made her flee Trent's party that night. Cruel words, overheard when Lee was on the veranda getting a breath of fresh air. Mrs Allingham had emerged with Trent, neither of them seeing her in the darkness, and, because Lee was intimidated by Mrs Allingham anyway, she had not revealed herself.

'Why did you invite that Dennison girl?' Trent's mother had asked in her haughtiest tone.

Trent's tone had been defensive. 'She's a nice kid, doesn't go to many parties.'

Mrs Allingham had sniffed. 'She's obviously starry-eyed about you. But she's not one of us, Trent, darling, and I wouldn't want you to get into trouble over her. Girls like that, you know, are always on the lookout to trap an eligible man.' She had added pointedly, 'As heir to Hilsborough you're a good catch.'

Trent had protested in amazement, 'She's a seventeen-year-old kid, Mother, who has a passion for motorbikes, that's all! I occasionally take her for a spin on mine. She's not my girlfriend! I invited her because she's off to Melbourne tomorrow to start her nursing training. I dare say I won't see her again for a long time, if ever.' The dismissiveness in his tone had made it so much worse. He'd only asked her to the party to give her a treat.

His mother had said with relief, 'Well, that's good news.' She had added sharply, 'Nevertheless, your father and I would prefer that you didn't associate with girls like her. There are plenty of suitable girls you can take out. We hope you'll marry one of them and settle down soon.'

Trent had laughed. 'I've got other things to do, Mother, before I even think about marriage, as you well know.'

She had said stiffly, 'We won't talk about that now, Trent. This is a social occasion and I don't want it spoiled by arguments.'

Listening in the darkness, Lee had struggled with anger and humiliation, and had not, of course, understood the signifance of all their remarks. Mrs Allingham had swept back inside, but Trent, strolling along the veranda, had discovered Lee before she could escape. He had realised that she must have heard, which only made her feel all the more humiliated. She had flung some wild words at him and fled, running blindly across the lawns until she came to the summerhouse, where she had hidden. But Trent had found her there too, and when she had sobbed her heart out and he had assured her that he didn't care what his mother thought, in the height of shared emotional states they had made love.

What Trent had in mind for the day was bushwalking in a scenic area of the Otways. 'I used to come here when I was a boy,' he told Lee. 'I'm hoping it hasn't changed much.'

'Unless they've logged the bit you remember, I dare say it won't have,' she said.

They left the car and, with Trent carrying a large backpack, set off along one of the bush trails. Trent set a brisk pace, and as they had to walk single file for most of the time there was little opportunity for conversation. When there was, Shannon made sure it was between her and Trent.

They eventually found the spot that Trent remembered, high up with a panoramic view across the ranges to the ocean.

'I'm starving,' Shannon announced. 'Can we have lunch now?' She grinned cheekily at Trent.

He spread the rug which had been rolled up on top of the backpack and Lee unpacked the food. Edna

Powis's picnic lunch was lavish and satisfying. After they had eaten, Shannon and Trent went off to bird-watch and take photographs, and Lee lay back and stared at the sky, feeling extraordinarily content. But how many outings like this could she bear? It was going to tear her apart.

The new maternity department was abuzz on Monday morning. Two births were imminent, and one was presenting a potential problem because the baby was in the breech position.

Lee returned to her office from supervising the care being given to both women to be informed that A and E had just accepted a new admission and a bed was urgently needed.

'We're flat out,' she said, raking her hair. 'Can you keep her there for half an hour? I'll organise something by then.'

Trent, having checked on the two patients in the labour ward, looked into her office as she put the phone down.

'You look frazzled,' he said. 'Cheer up. Everything's under control. Mrs Porter will pop hers on schedule with no problems, and Mrs Sheridan's X-ray indicates that a Caesarean may not be necessary.'

'She'll be relieved,' said Lee.

He nodded. 'So am I. An episiotomy should do the trick. I've told her what it means—a small incision below the vaginal opening to facilitate the birth without tearing, which will be easily stitched afterwards. She's naturally rather anxious, so you might like to confirm it just to reassure her. Keep an eye on her, and call me if there's the least cause for concern. Her GP will be here shortly.' He crossed to her desk and looked steadily at her, smiling ruefully. 'Why do the little beasts sometimes present the wrong way round?'

'Nature being contrary?' Lee suggested.

'The system isn't perfect,' Trent said in all seriousness. 'There's so much that can go wrong, but fortunately it doesn't most of the time.'

Lee remembered her new patient and dragged her eyes away from his. 'A and E just rang. They have an emergency for us—a woman with antepartum haemorrhage. They're sending her up in half an hour.'

He looked outraged. 'Half an hour?'

'We're flat out,' she explained. 'I can't get a bed ready in less time.' She added pointedly, 'We haven't got the extra staff we were promised yet, you know.'

He accepted her explanation grudgingly. 'Well, be ready as soon as you can. Meanwhile I'll go down and see her.'

In twenty minutes the bed for the new patient was ready, and Lee phoned down to the casualty department.

'Dr Allingham's on his way up with the patient,' she was told, and as she hung up he burst through the door.

'Have you got the bed ready?' he rapped out, impatient now.

'Yes. Room two,' Lee told him, adding, 'No op?'

'At this stage I don't think surgical intervention is called for,' he said. 'The foetus is normal. It's possible she'll go full term.'

After the patient had been settled, Trent continued discussion of her condition with Lee. It was a trait she appreciated, one not always seen in doctors. They gave orders, and expected them to be obeyed without question, but only some, like Trent, credited nurses with real medical knowledge. She'd even heard complaints that some doctors scoffed at the new system of college training for nurses, saying it gave them ideas above their station.

'It's not easy to diagnose precisely what the problem is,' he confessed. 'She's losing a fair amount of blood, but she says she doesn't have any pain.'

'How far gone is she? About thirty weeks?'

'Thirty-three, she says.'

'Is it placenta praevia?' suggested Lee.

He nodded. 'Most likely. So far there's no sign of pre-eclamptic toxaemia, though.' He glanced at her sharply. 'You know what placenta praevia means precisely?'

Without thinking, Lee said feelingly, 'I ought to! I had the same problem. I was sure I was going to lose the baby.' She clamped her lips together, regretting the personal admission.

He said softly, 'Did you want to?'

'No. Not then. Not after all those months of having her a part of me. I couldn't wait to see her—or him; I didn't know what sex it was—and I was terribly afraid that it would all have been in vain. . .' She drew in a long breath and let it out slowly.

'It was a natural birth, though?'

Lee wished she hadn't aroused his curiosity. It was hardly the time to be discussing her pregnancy. 'Yes, I was lucky.'

'There's so much I don't know about you,' Trent murmured.

Lee averted her gaze. 'You were asking me about the condition placenta praevia,' she went on. 'There are several ways in which the placenta can become separated from the wall of the uterus as it stretches late in pregnancy. Depending on the site of the detachment, the blood loss will be small or profuse. . .'

Trent reached for her wrist. 'Hold it! You don't have to give me chapter and verse! I'm not testing you!'

Lee turned her arm from his grasp and moved a step away. 'It couldn't be just polyps, or vaginitis, I suppose?'

'I don't think so, but I'll examine her more thoroughly tomorrow, when she's settled down. Meanwhile, regular obs, please, of pulse, blood-pressure—especially blood-pressure—and measure the blood loss. You'd better have her urine tested for protein, and have a blood cross-match done in case a transfusion is necessary.'

'X-rays?' Lee queried.

Trent considered briefly. 'Not at this stage. We may need to have soft tissue X-rays to show the placenta, but I'll keep that as an option for the moment—until I've eliminated superficial causes for the bleeding at least.' He caught her chin in his hand and made her look at him. 'You suffered a lot to have Shannon, didn't you?'

Lee felt her knees begin to shake. 'No more than a lot of mothers, a lot less than some.'

'But you were only eighteen,' he said, shaking his head. 'Just a kid!'

'You grow up fast when you have responsibilities thrust on you.' She added loyally, 'And I had Callie and her family, don't forget.'

'Nice people,' he said. He was searching her face as though trying to read the thoughts behind her words.

'I was lucky,' she said again.

His grip on her jaw tightened. 'Lee, you can't marry Michael——'

'Trent, please, I don't want to discuss it,' Lee protested. 'I don't bring my personal life to work. And I'm too busy anyway.'

His hand dropped to his side. 'Besides which, it's none of my damned business, except that Shannon is my daughter, and I don't see Michael Farrow as a suitable father for her!'

'Shhh! Trent, *please*. . .' Lee begged. He marched out of the door with an abruptness that left her feeling that her face had been slapped.

By lunchtime both the mothers in labour had been delivered of healthy babies, without undue fuss, and Lee went to lunch feeling relieved. There was a slight air of euphoria clinging to her which still came with the bringing of new life into the world and seeing the happiness it created. No matter how many babies she saw born, she always experienced a personal thrill as she saw the downy head appear, then the small prune-like face and tiny perfect limbs, and finally heard the reassuring wail as the lungs took their first unaided breath.

'People talk about the miracle of birth,' she said to Zena, who joined her at the table in the canteen, 'but it happens too often to be a miracle! And yet. . .'

Zena swallowed a mouthful of pizza. 'I know. It's a perfectly normal, natural, precision event, cleverly devised by old mother nature not to go wrong too often, but I get a funny little lump in my throat too. Well, not so much now I'm on Gynae, of course.' She laughed. 'It's our maternal instincts, Lee. Every baby we see delivered we imagine is ours. I guess we're envious.' She sighed dreamily. 'I wonder what sort of babies Andrew's would be.'

'That might depend on the mother. Now, if she had

dark hair, blue eyes, and an ever so slightly turned up nose,' Lee said teasingly, describing Zena, 'they might be rather cute!'

'I should be so lucky,' groaned Zena. Her eyes lit up mischievously. 'I wonder what Trent's babies would look like. I bet they'd be incredibly beautiful or handsome regardless of their mother. I bet he's got dominant genes!' She looked slyly at Lee. 'Do you fancy him, Lee?'

Lee took care with her reply. 'Wouldn't do me much good if I did, would it? He has more glamorous fish to fry than mere nurses.'

Zena put her elbows on the table, linked her fingers and rested her chin on them. She observed Lee closely. 'You haven't mentioned Michael much lately. Are you still seeing him?'

Lee was carefully casual. 'Yes, of course.'

The phone was ringing as she arrived home that day. It was Michael.

'You're late,' he said. 'Hard day?'

'No, not really. Quite exhilarating, in fact. I stopped for groceries on the way home.'

'So you're not worn out from tramping the wards for once?'

'No. . .' Lee saw the direction of his words, but could think of no way to forestall him.

'Let's go somewhere for dinner, then,' he suggested. 'I heard today about a new country house restaurant that's just opened. One of the reps told me about it. What do you say? Shall we try it?'

Lee was ashamed of her reluctance. She said, 'All right. I don't feel much like cooking tonight.'

The weather was cooler now, especially in the evenings, so Lee wore a blue linen suit and softly draped white blouse. Michael looked suave in a grey suit and maroon tie, and, stealing glances at him as they drove, Lee tried to see him as a husband. Did she care enough about him to marry him? She would never love him as she loved Trent Allingham, but if she married him she would try. But before he got around to asking her, she must tell him about Shannon. It wasn't fair not to. She would definitely do so tonight, she decided.

But somehow the right moment never arrived. There were too many people around, too many waiters hovering, and the tables were not private enough. Maybe going home in the car. . . But on the way home, it was Michael who did all the talking, as he had done for most of the evening. Finally he said, 'You're very quiet this evening, Lee.'

'Am I?'

'You've hardly said a word.'

'Sorry.'

He parked in the garage forecourt and turned to her. 'Lee. . .' She was in his arms before she realised it, and he was kissing her with an unusual fervour. 'Lee,' he said, lifting his head, 'let's get married.'

Lee was caught completely off guard. 'Michael. . .'

He held her close. 'Lee, there isn't anyone else, is there?'

She swallowed hard. 'No, of course not.'

He tucked tendrils of hair behind her ears. 'Let's make it soon, darling.'

'But, Michael, I don't know. . .' She was unprepared, and didn't know what to say.

He went on persuasively, 'You know I'm keen to get elected to the council—well, I've been asked to put up at the election in July.'

'I'm sure you'll win,' Lee heard herself saying. 'You've always been very active in community work.'

He warmed to his theme. 'It'll be good experience if I do. Lee, I don't want to spend all my life in this backwater. I hope I may get into state parliament one day, maybe even go to Canberra.' His eyes glinted with ambition, as he held her tightly. 'Lee, I know you'll be a credit to me!'

Foolishly, as she now realised, Lee had never pictured herself in that role, and she instinctively retreated from it. And at the same time it was clear to her that there was no need to tell him about Shannon, because she knew she couldn't marry Michael. She couldn't marry any man without love.

'Well,' he said, 'shall we set a date?'

Lee felt stone cold inside. 'Michael, I'm sorry. . .' she began, stumbling over her words.

The lines between his eyes deepened. 'You mean—no? But, Lee, I thought. . .'

It was obvious he had been confident she would say yes, and he couldn't understand her flat refusal.

Lee hated herself, but she had to spell it out. 'I can't marry you, Michael. I'm sorry if I've seemed to mislead you, but the truth is I'm not in love with you. And I'm not sure you are with me.'

He gave a short derisive laugh. 'Come now, Lee, we're both grown people. We don't make major decisions about our lives based on romance!'

She moistened her lips nervously. She didn't want to argue with him because he didn't understand. He stared at her for a moment, then said, half angrily, 'I see. Well, there's no more to be said, then.'

'I'm truly sorry, Michael,' Lee murmured again.

He didn't argue any further, and she said a hasty goodnight.

CHAPTER NINE

'YOU'RE not going to believe this,' Zena said, as she slid into a chair opposite Lee at lunchtime. Her cheeks were pink and her eyes sparkled.

Lee looked at her plate piled high with chips, and the lavishly decorated slice of cream sponge she'd selected for dessert. 'I thought you were on a diet?'

'I'm celebrating!'

Lee raised an eyebrow. 'Oh? A legacy, lottery win? What?'

Zena tossed her dark hair. It was obvious she was trying not to let a smile break right across her face. She dived into her pocket and thrust a small red velvet box at Lee. 'I'm engaged. To Andrew,' she whispered. 'You're the first to know.'

Lee was stunned. 'But I thought. . .' She opened the box and caught her breath at the solitaire diamond ring nestling in its cream satin bed.

'So did I,' said Zena. 'But Andrew's a real dark horse. Apparently he's been in love with me for ages, but he thought I wasn't interested in him, so he pretended to be indifferent, and there was I doing precisely the same thing. Maddening, isn't it?'

A pang of envy cut into Lee's pleasure at the news. Although she knew she had done the right thing, she still felt a little raw about rejecting Michael's proposal.

'So how did you finally discover the mutual attraction?' she asked.

Zena laughed. 'It was classic! We were shorthanded

and I happened to be clearing away a patient's tea tray. My beeper went and I rushed out of the room just as he was about to go in and we collided. I dropped the tray and we both scrambled to collect the crockery, which fortunately wasn't smashed, and we sort of suddenly stopped and looked at each other, eyeball to eyeball. Lee, it was the corniest cliché. He said in a funny sort of voice, "Zena. . .?" and I went all mushy and said, "Andrew. . ." Then he said, "Are you hurt?" and helped me up. He handed me the tray and there were these weird electric shocks zooming through me. I was shaking like a leaf, and I fled.'

Lee was having difficulty controlling her amusement at Zena's graphic telling. 'And then?'

Zena's eyes were dreamy. 'He came along to my office later in the day to see how I was. He was *so* concerned, I couldn't help acting a bit fragile. I was dying to tell you, but I thought it wouldn't last. Until last Saturday when he said we ought to get engaged.'

Lee handed back the ring box. She squeezed Zena's hand. 'It's wonderful news, Zena, and I'm really happy for you,' she said. 'I'm so glad that it's come out all right after all.'

Zena pocketed the ring. 'We thought we'd have a small celebration party on Thursday night. At my place. Can you come?'

'Love to,' Lee said. 'When are you planning to get married?'

'Soon.' Zena blushed. 'Andrew's not one to let the grass grow under his feet.'

'So it seems!' Lee pointed to Zena's plate. 'You're not eating your chips.'

Her friend pulled a rueful face. 'I'm not hungry.' She giggled. 'It must be love.'

Lee grinned. 'Well, I'll pass the chips, but I hate to see that sponge going to waste.'

Zena pushed the confection across the table and sighed. 'I shouldn't anyway. You can afford to, with your figure.'

'And I'm not in love,' Lee joked. She wished it were true. Loving Trent had not spoiled her appetite, but perhaps it would if she were ever in the same blissful situation as Zena, having her love returned. Oh, why was real happiness so elusive?

The rest of the day was uneventful for once. After lunch Lee looked in on a baby-bathing session where Isobel, the new senior staff nurse, was instructing both the mother and the junior, Rose. All, including the baby, seemed to be enjoying themselves.

As she turned to leave, Lee found Trent looking over her shoulder.

'I suppose you wish all days could be as trouble-free as today,' he said.

'Don't you?' The emotional charge she received from him was powerful.

'Yes, except that I always wonder what Nemesis hangs over our complacency.'

'You sound like Zena!' she laughed.

He walked along to the mothers' day-room with her, saying, 'You'll be going to Andrew's and Zena's engagement party?'

'Yes, of course.'

'I'll pick you up,' he offered. 'You can't ride your bike in a party dress.'

She could think of no reason to refuse. 'Thanks.'

He paused outside the day-room door. 'Mrs Lincoln has me a bit worried,' he told her.

The patient he mentioned had been admitted two

days ago. She was in her early forties and had a heart condition. Lee raised a questioning eyebrow.

'I want the cardiologist to see her.' He raked his hair briefly as he often did when anxious. 'She ought not to be having another child.'

'Shall I ask Dr Prentice to see her?' Lee asked.

Trent nodded. 'As soon as he can. Let me know when he arrives, please, Lee.'

His eyes flicked over her, and a faint smile hovered around his mouth. His scrutiny unnerved her and set her heart racing past normal.

On Thursday evening, Trent called for her promptly at seven. There was to be an informal buffet, Zena had told everyone, around eight.

It was raining. Lee flung a raincoat over her mint-green dress and hoisted an umbrella to run to the car. Breathless, she flopped into the passenger-seat, and shook as much of the water off her umbrella as she could outside before dumping it, on Trent's instruction, in the back.

'What a night!' she exclaimed, peering through the windscreen, which the wipers were hardly fast enough to clear.

'Just the night for a party,' he remarked. He seemed a little preoccupied and didn't say much more on the way to Zena's house.

The party was lively and Lee enjoyed herself. It was not often that the staff of Shearwater Community Hospital let their hair down in a get-together. Mostly they seemed to keep their social life separate from work.

Lee enjoyed having time to chat to people she saw often enough but seldom had the chance to talk to. She made a point of not hanging around Trent, and couldn't help noticing that he quickly acquired female admirers. Away from the wards and operating rooms, without even the minimum formality the hospital demanded, everyone was more at ease, especially juniors with seniors, nurses with doctors.

As the evening wore on, the noise level rose, laughter increased and the music was turned up. Lee began to develop a headache. When Trent suddenly appeared at her side and said, 'Have you had enough?' Lee was sure he must be able to read her mind.

'Does that mean you have?' she queried.

'I'm not a great partygoer,' he confessed. 'And you look as though you need an analgesic and to be tucked up in bed.' He smoothed the frown marks between her eyes and let his fingers move soothingly across her brow. Lee briefly closed here eyes. It was bliss.

She opened them and smiled. 'You've been watching me. Diagnosis from a distance—that's clever! As a matter of fact I do have a slight headache. I shouldn't have had red wine.'

He caught hold of her arm decisively. 'Let's go.'

Zena gave Lee a sly look when she told her they were leaving, but she didn't tease.

The rain had eased to a light drizzle and the streets were more or less deserted. Neon signs were reflected garishly in the still streaming gutters and roadways and the air was cool. It was warm in the car, however, and Lee could easily have curled up in her seat and gone to sleep. But the journey home was no more than five or six minutes.

Back at Dennison's, Trent insisted on seeing Lee to her door, where she thanked him and said goodnight. She flung off her raincoat and went to the kitchen to make coffee. She had barely plugged the kettle in when the doorbell rang.

Slipping the chain on the door, she opened it warily. Callers at this time of night were rare. Trent stood there, holding out her umbrella. Lee stared at it for a moment before the penny dropped.

'Oh, it's mine! How stupid of me to forget it!' she exclaimed.

'How clever of me to remember!' he joked.

She felt silly talking to him through the narrow slit. She slipped the chain off and opened it wider, taking the umbrella from him. 'Thanks.' She hesitated, then said, 'I'm just making coffee, if you'd like some.'

'Thanks, I wouldn't mind,' he said, stepping inside and closing the door behind him, as Lee headed back to the kitchen.

Seated at her kitchen table, he asked, 'How's the head?'

'Better already. It was the loud music, I think.'

Lee made the coffee and suggested they drink it in the comfort of the living-room. Trent carried the tray and she motioned him to the couch, while selecting an armchair herself. Her headache had eased, but her awareness of the man who now sprawled comfortably on her sofa was as acute as ever, and it was a different kind of ache she felt.

They talked in snatches, like strangers, awkward with each other, uneasy, as though there were things each wanted to say but couldn't. Finally Trent rose to go, and Lee stood up too.

'Thanks for taking me to the party,' she said.

He was close, less than an arm's length away, and she had to fight a strong desire to slide into his arms. Her fight was short-lived. Trent moved the one step necessary to bring them together, and drew her against him, holding her head against his chest, resting his cheek against her hair.

'Why do we deny it when we both know there's a powerful attraction between us?' he murmured, tilting her head and holding her face in his hands. 'What's the point of inflicting torture on each other, when there could be so much pleasure?' Skilful hands caressed her until she wanted to fling off the party dress and feel his skin touching hers.

It was madness, and it was inevitable. Just once, she thought. Would it be so wrong to experience the joy of making love to him just once more? Surely that was what she needed to do, to find out if making love to Trent was as glorious as she had once believed, or whether memory had deceived her. They were both older now. She had changed from a naïve teenager to a mature woman. Maybe she would find Trent was no one special now. Maybe she would lay a ghost to rest. . .

But these were the rational arguments, they were not the real reason she clung to him and let him push her gently down on the couch and with swift, expert movements remove her clothes. She accepted his lovemaking because her whole being cried out for him and would no longer be denied. Love was the reason she wanted him now. Love was the reason she had always wanted him. His talents as a lover, although remembered as something special, had never had much to do with it.

Trent looked at her naked form for a moment, sitting beside her, caressing her from shoulder to thigh, bending his lips to her breasts and brushing them across her midriff. 'You're lovely, Lee,' he whispered hoarsely. He touched the faint scar which the graze on her thigh had left, stroking it tenderly, touching it with his lips. 'Your skin is so satiny smooth. . .'

His voice broke slightly, and he stood up. In a few seconds his clothes had joined hers and his warm body was covering hers, torso to torso, pelvis to pelvis, thigh to thigh, everywhere his skin met hers, electrifying her nerve-ends. Her legs parted and her body arched when his demanded it, and for a moment she thought it would all go wrong. She felt as inexperienced now as when she was seventeen, as naïve in the ways of lovemaking as she had been then, but Trent was skilful and guided her gently at first, then with a power and strength that brought her swiftly to the ultimate fiery consummation her body had been yearning for. She heard a voice cry out and realised it was her own. Tears dampened her cheeks and she didn't even try to brush them away. Trent was now so much more than memories. He was warm, vibrant reality.

His grey eyes, darkened by desire, were watching her when she opened hers. A finger lightly brushed the tears from her cheeks. 'Lovely woman,' he whispered. Twelve years ago in the darkness of a summerhouse, Lee remembered, he had dried her tears and whispered, 'Lovely girl.'

'Trent. . .' She could find no words to say, so she told him, 'I—I don't know what to say. . .'

He covered her mouth with his, kissing her slowly with the tenderness of passion spent. 'Don't say anything,' he recommended, smiling at her. 'We've said it all, haven't we?'

Had they? Lee was afraid they had not, but she did not have the strength to spoil this moment. 'Are you cold?' she asked.

'Not yet, but I guess we soon will be. Which way is your bedroom?'

He rolled away from her, stood and lifted her up in his arms and carried her swiftly down the passage to her room. Without switching on the light, because the room was dimly lit by street lights shining through the curtains, he set her on her feet, still holding her close with one strong arm around her, as though afraid she might run away, and dragged back the bedclothes. Lee shivered slightly. They fell into the bed together and she felt returning warmth as the bedclothes were pulled back over them. They kissed for long satisfying moments, taking pleasure in their entwined closeness, and in a little while Trent pulled her on top of him and they made love again, with less urgency but a deeper exploration of each other's needs. Then, tightly held in his arms, Lee nuzzled close against him again and fell asleep.

She woke to the aroma of coffee. Muzzily she sat up, discovered her nakedness and drew the sheet up to her chin. Trent came in, with a tray. He was wearing her floral dressing-gown, but the edges didn't quite meet across his broad frame, let alone cross over. Lee chuckled at the ludicrous sight and he pretended not to know what she found amusing.

'You! In my dressing-gown. Drag doesn't suit you.' She glanced at the clock. It was five a.m. 'You're an early bird,' she quavered, flushing as the memory of last night's lovemaking returned with palpable reality.

'You start at eight, don't you?' said Trent, putting the tray on the bedside table.

'I'm usually there by seven-thirty. It only takes me an hour to get ready, ten minutes to ride to work.'

'So we have time to talk,' he said, and sat on the bed, taking her free hand in his.

'Talk?' Lee sipped the hot coffee which he had made strong, black and sweet. He must have noticed how she liked it.

He nodded. He took a gulp of his own coffee and, clasping her free hand, said, 'Give me a chance, Lee.'

'A chance? For what?'

'To make up for lost time. Marry me, Lee.'

His eyes were soft, desire rekindling in them, and she felt herself responding. But she shook her head slowly.

His face darkened. 'Lee. . .' he said almost angrily, squeezing her fingers till they hurt.

Lee felt a sudden wave of sympathy. He was in as invidious a position as she was. 'Trent, I'm sorry. . .'

He leaned forward and kissed her, then took her cup and saucer and placed them back on the tray beside his own. He drew her close and the sheet fell away, as did the dressing-gown, so their bodies touched with tingling contact. His eyes bored into hers.

'After last night you can't still want to marry Michael Farrow.'

Lee looked at him, loving him, resisting him, although every fibre of her being wanted to do whatever he wanted. She stayed silent, while he traced the shape of her nose and mouth with a feather-light fingertip. He had planned last night, she thought. He had wanted to show her he was better at lovemaking than Michael.

'A night of passion isn't love,' she said. 'And neither does sharing a daughter mean we're in love.'

Trent held her fiercely. 'I'm in love with you.'

'You have to say that now.' Lee took his hand and stroked it, and her touch almost sent him wild again. He'd assumed too much, read too much into her generously uninhibited lovemaking, her totally natural enjoyment of their union. It had never been like that with anyone else. He looked desperately into her green eyes, so honest, so guileless, and he read the regret with a sinking heart.

She moistened dry lips hesitantly. 'Trent, be realistic. We're very different, we come from and move in very different worlds. You can't just ignore that! You don't have to pretend to be in love with me! I won't stop you from seeing Shannon if you want to—we'll tell her, if you like—but marriage doesn't mend mistakes.'

He was withdrawn suddenly. 'Are you saying that making love that night in the summerhouse at Hilsborough was a mistake? That making love last night was a mistake too?'

Lee felt the problems settling over her like a dark cloud. 'Yes—no—I don't know, Trent. But would you have asked me to marry you if you hadn't discovered about Shannon? Of course you wouldn't. You'd have had a brief affair with me perhaps if I'd been willing, but I'm not the kind of woman you would marry, even if you wanted to get married. I'm too ordinary, still a bit of a tomboy tearing around on a motorbike, not like those sophisticated women you know—like Francine.'

He jerked back impatiently. 'For heaven's sake, Lee! You're not still brooding over that old hurt, are you? I thought I'd persuaded you then that it didn't make a hoot of difference to me who or what you were, that I despised my mother because she was such a frightful snob.'

'Yes, you did persuade me, but Trent, can you honestly say that if things had been different, if we'd both stayed in Shearwater, if I hadn't been pregnant, you would have remotely considered marrying me?'

'Which makes me as much of a snob as my mother.'

'No, but. . . Oh, please try to understand,' Lee begged desperately.

'Lee. . .oh, Lee, what a stubborn little mule you are,' Trent sighed, gathering her into his arms. 'To me you're the most wonderful woman I've ever met, and that's all that matters. You went through hell and brought up my daughter instead of abandoning her to someone else, and I love you for it. . .' He went on softly, 'I fell in love with you that night, but the timing was all wrong, and you were so young.'

She said, 'Don't forget how relieved you were when you knew you wouldn't have to marry me. It had given you a fright, hadn't it? And ever after you were always very careful.'

'If you hadn't been so distant when I called you. . .'

She was suddenly frightened of the commitment he was urging her towards, even though it was what she most wanted in the world. If she believed him it might only be because she wanted to.

'You only want to marry me because of Shannon,' she insisted. 'I think you're trying to kid yourself as well as me.'

'It's not just because of Shannon,' Trent said tightly, and challenged her, 'All right, say it straight out. Last night—it was just one of those things, is that what you mean? Physical attraction. Simple old sex. Right? Just an excusable lapse after a couple of glasses of wine too many. But don't pretend you're in love with Michael, because I don't believe it.'

Lee's tears welled up.

'Oh, Lee, darling. . .' Trent held her close again.

She sobbed against his bare chest, 'It's no good—it wouldn't last.'

He threaded his fingers through her hair. 'I promise you it will.'

'You can't promise that,' Lee said sadly. 'You know marriage isn't what you really want. If you'd been the marrying kind, Trent, you wouldn't still be single.' Her voice rose as she went on, 'And besides, *if* you marry anyone, it'll be someone like Francine, you know it will.'

'Don't be ridiculous!' He smiled at her and kissed her lips. 'Maybe I was just waiting to meet you again.'

'Rubbish. That's just romantic talk. It's not reality. You won't change, Trent. You're a bit bemused at the moment at the discovery that you have a daughter, that's understandable, but discovering you still want to go to bed with me doesn't mean we have to get married.'

'Think of Shannon. . .'

'I am thinking of Shannon. I want what's best for her. I don't want her to find a father and then lose him again, perhaps when she most needs his emotional support in her adolescent years.'

'And I don't want some other man bringing up my daughter!' Trent said vehemently. 'I don't want that pompous little pharmacist taking what should be my place.'

Lee swallowed hard. 'He won't be,' she said. 'I've already told him I can't marry him. I won't marry anyone, Trent. I think that's the best way.'

Trent stood up and paced to the window, his hands shoved in the pockets of her dressing-gown, his mouth a hard line, his jaw rigid. Lee slid down under the bedclothes.

'You can have a shower here, if you like,' she offered.

He turned and said savagely, 'Thanks very much! Thanks for your hospitality, Lee. Is that all you have to offer me?'

'I know it's hard for you to understand,' she sighed. 'I'm not sure I quite understand myself. I'm frightened, Trent, that's all. . . I'm frightened of what will happen to us. I'm scared of letting emotion win over good sense. And I don't want Shannon to be hurt.'

Trent came back and said less vehemently, 'Lee, when Shannon was conceived, you were young and vulnerable and I was in the midst of emotional uncertainties. I made a mess of things with my parents, and later I suppose I didn't try hard enough to become reconciled. I had a career to think about, and I was hurt at the way they'd treated me. I had pride too, so I went my own way, made a success of my life, but there was a lack, an emotional vacuum, the significance of which I didn't realise at the time.' He sat on the edge of the bed again and placed his hands on her bare shoulders. Lee quivered at his touch. 'It's true I was relieved when you told me there was nothing to worry about. It was another problem I didn't have to cope with. I didn't realise what had happened to me that night with you.' He looked at her with mute appeal for a long moment. 'Lee, I'm trying to reconcile my life now,' he said quietly. 'Coming back to Shearwater and Hilsborough is part of it. Coming back to my roots and finding you seemed like fate taking a hand. Lee, don't reject me, please. Think about it. . .give me a chance . . .to make amends, to make you happy, you and Shannon.'

He kissed her mouth tenderly, and Lee was unable to help herself responding. When his hands slid under the bedclothes and began caressing her, she muttered, 'I have to get up and go to work.'

'It's only six,' he said, nuzzling her neck and beginning to trail kisses along her collarbone and into the cleft between her breasts. 'Plenty of time.'

Lee needed no persuading. When he lifted the bedclothes and slid in beside her, discarding her dressing-gown as he did so, she sighed deeply with pleasure and for some time her brain refused to deal with the problems that confronted her.

In the end they both had a frantic rush to shower and dress, and there was no time for breakfast and none for talking. As they left the house Lee glanced up and down Jacaranda Parade and wondered if anyone would have noticed that the Mercedes parked at the far end of the garage forecourt had been there all night, and if so if they would speculate or merely think it was in for servicing.

As she wheeled her motorbike out of the service bay where she kept it, Trent was about to get into the car, but hesitated and walked across to her.

'I forgot to mention,' he said, 'that I'll be away for a few days. I've got to go to Sydney today—obstetrics conference. I expect to be back about next Wednesday.'

Lee tensed. 'That's a long conference.'

'The conference is three days, but I have other business to attend to.' Rather reluctantly, she thought, he added, 'I have to see Francine to discuss a few things about the refurbishing of Hilsborough. She seems to think money's no object!'

'Where will you stay?' Lee asked.

'I still have my apartment,' he told her. 'I don't mean to sell it. It's handy to have a place of one's own to go to.'

Yes, I'm sure, Lee thought, imagining the long, lonely times she might have to endure while he was away, if she married him. The times when he needed his freedom. 'Have a good time, Trent,' she said. She revved the bike's engine and roared off towards the hospital, with Francine Kennedy's beautiful face and elegant clothes taunting her.

CHAPTER TEN

To LEE, the weekend stretched interminably ahead. In order to keep from brooding over what Trent might be doing in Sydney—with Francine—she spent most of the time making plans for the school holidays, which were only a week away.

'Why should I care what he does in Sydney?' she reminded herself more than once.

Lee looked forward to school holidays as they gave her so much longer with her daughter. They had always got along well, so, mulling over what Trent had said about Shannon wanting to live with her, perhaps, she thought, this holiday might be the right time to broach the subject. But if Shannon were to live with her in Shearwater, she would have to explain to her about the garage and why she had never told her about Max. Lee still did not relish the prospect of the gossip that her suddenly producing an eleven-year-old daughter would be bound to cause, but, as Trent had said, she could not keep her hidden away forever. The simple solution was, of course, to leave Shearwater. Maybe the time had come to do that. Sell the garage and motel and move back to Melbourne where she could start afresh and be anonymous. Lee faced that prospect without real enthusiasm. Oddly enough, she liked Shearwater, was happy there. It was still 'home'.

It wasn't until after lunch at the Morrises', when they were washing the dishes, that Callie dropped the bombshell that was to force Lee into the course she had been considering rather more precipitately than she had expected.

'Are you all right, Callie?' Lee asked. 'You look as though you've got something on your mind.' From Callie's quick glance, she sensed that bad news was to come. 'What's the matter?' Her stomach clenched at the thought that Callie might be ill.

'I'm not feeling the best,' Callie admitted, 'but it's nothing physical, just a bit of a shock to the system, I suppose, and wondering how to tell you.'

'Tell me what?'

Callie paused and turned to face Lee. 'We're leaving, Lee. Nick's been offered a job in Brisbane, back in his old department at CSIRO.'

Lee was dumbfounded. Callie went on, 'You know it's been difficult lately to make ends meet on the farm, with the recession and all that. Well, Nick's afraid if he doesn't do something now he'll soon be too old, and when this opportunity arose he felt he had to take it. The kids' schooling is a factor. . .'

Lee was too stunned to say more than, 'I understand. Of course I do.' The implications were already crowding her brain. Callie's news was a shock, but perhaps not such a traumatic development as it might have been.

Callie looked miserable. 'Lee, I'm not sure I want to go. It's a big upheaval. We haven't told the kids yet. I wanted to tell you first, to discuss what you want to do. You and Shannon could come to Brisbane. . .'

It was a moment of truth for Lee. She saw that she had reached a crossroads and must make a decision. And because of her previous deliberations, it was easy to make. Now was the time to assume full responsibility for her daughter and stop depending on Callie and her family. She would not trail along after them. She would stand on her own two feet.

'I don't think so,' she said slowly, automatically drying the plates Callie had gone back to washing. 'As a matter of fact, I've been thinking that maybe it's time Shannon and I started living together and getting to know one another better. In fact, I've been thinking of moving back to Melbourne.'

It was Callie's turn to be astonished. She looked at Lee sharply. 'What about Trent?' she queried.

'It's nothing to do with him.'

Callie was aghast. 'But, Lee. . .'

Lee forced herself to be hard. 'He's Shannon's father, that's all. The novelty of being a father will soon wear off, Callie. Men like Trent don't really want family responsibilities.'

'So there's no chance of your marrying him?' Callie ventured without hope.

'There never was. None at all.'

Callie looked upset. 'What about Michael?'

Lee shook her head, forcing a laugh. 'He asked me to marry him, but I can't really see myself as a politician's wife.'

That made Callie smile. 'He really is serious about it, is he? Is that why you turned him down?'

'No, not really.'

'You weren't in love with him, were you?'

Lee shrugged. 'I suppose not, and it was clear he wasn't in love with me. When he proposed, he never even mentioned it. I think I'll stick to the single life, Callie. Relationships get too complicated.' She told her friend what Shannon had said to Trent about living with her. 'She'll enjoy living in Melbourne,' she said, 'and now Dad's gone, there's no reason for me to stay in Shearwater.'

Relief spread across her friend's face. 'I've been so worried about you,' Callie confessed. 'I've been lying awake at night. . .'

'Oh, Callie, I'm sorry,' Lee said. 'You should have told me sooner.'

'I couldn't until we were sure. I felt terrible about it, as though we were abandoning you and Shannon.'

'Of course you aren't!' Lee hastened to reassure her. 'In fact it's just the catalyst I need.' She asked, 'When are you leaving?'

Callie looked distraught. 'Nick wants us all to go up for the school holidays so we'll have time to look around for a house together, decide on schools for the children and generally get the feel of the place. It'll be a rush, and I'll have to come back later to pack up the rest of our gear and see about selling the farm. . .' She looked at Lee with appeal. 'I'm wondering if I can cope!'

'If anyone can, you can, Callie,' Lee assured her. Her brain was working fast. 'Shannon and I are going to Melbourne for the holidays. We'll find a place to live and I'll resign from the hospital and get a job in Melbourne.'

Callie looked doubtful. 'You're being very good about this, Lee.'

'In a way I'm glad it's happened,' Lee said thoughtfully. 'It was time for me to make some decisions, Callie.' She gave her friend a hug. 'But I'll miss you. And Nick and the kids. We both will.'

'No more than we'll miss you,' said Callie, her eyes misty.

Now that Lee had been told the Morrises' plans,

Callie and Nick told their children, and the rest of the afternoon was spent discussing both their futures and Lee and Shannon's. To Lee's relief, Shannon was eager to go to Melbourne to live, even though that would mean leaving the farm. Lee promised that they would find agistment for Pastry and that she would still be able to ride him.

Shannon had plans too. 'We can come up to Brisbane for our next holidays,' she declared confidently, then insisted, 'For Christmas too!'

As Lee was leaving, Callie flung her arms around her friend. 'I'll *miss* you!' she said, a sob in her voice already.

Lee felt choked too. 'Me too,' she whispered. 'You've been a friend in a million, Callie, you and Nick and the kids. I don't know what Shannon and I would have done without you.'

'We'll still be around if you need us,' Callie said with a smile. 'We're only going to Brisbane, not Mars!'

Feeling guilty because she had no intention of telling Trent her plans, Lee wished he would stay away longer so she would not have to see him before she left, but he'd said he would be back on Wednesday, and he was.

It proved to be a hectic day. A flu epidemic was keeping the wards shorthanded, and Lee found herself flying from one crisis to another and helping out with tasks which were normally the duty of other nurses. She barely had a moment to enquire if Trent had enjoyed his conference.

When she did, he answered briefly, 'Yes, thanks.'

The look he gave her made her clench inside. She longed to be gone from Shearwater, but she also dreaded the moment of going. How was she going to bear being away from him?

'How was Francine?' she asked.

'Fine. She's coming down this weekend.' He wasn't cool exactly, but definitely distant. 'It's school holidays next week, isn't it? Going away?'

'Ye-es,' Lee answered shakily. 'I'm taking Shannon to Melbourne.'

A faint smile accompanied a tuneless rendition of, 'How're you goin' to keep 'em down on the farm. . .?' but the humour sounded forced.

She smiled back and her heart turned over. Would she ever get over this man?

Trent turned his attention back to the case notes in his hand. 'Mrs Forbes says she's allergic to penicillin, but there's nothing here.' He stabbed the sheet and looked accusingly at her. There was nothing personal now in his manner, only brisk clinical detachment. He was telling her, Lee knew, that they were merely colleagues again. Anything personal between them was over. She should have been glad of it, but she wanted to run somewhere, hide and cry her eyes out.

'I'm sorry. It must have been missed.'

'Important facts about a patient should *never* be missed,' he said in the tone she had rarely heard him use. 'That's the kind of slipshod behaviour that can cause disasters.'

Lee bit her lip. 'I didn't. . .'

He thrust the sheaf of notes at her impatiently. 'I don't suppose you did, but you're in charge of this department, Lee. It's your responsibility to see it's run efficiently.'

He had never spoken to her so harshly before, and she felt diminished because what he had said was right, even if it was impossible to check every questionnaire herself.

'I'll speak to the nurse concerned,' she said.

She did not see him again that day, and on Thursday he was occupied for most of the day with a long gynae list. There were two deliveries which Andrew attended and no major problems.

One more day, Lee thought, as she rode to work on Friday morning. She had decided to hire a car and she had already packed and loaded some of her gear. She had come to Shearwater with only meagre possessions, and was leaving with not much more. What she couldn't take now, and Shannon's stuff, would be collected later. So far she had not thought too much about selling Dennison's, although that was what she would ultimately do, she had decided.

She walked into the maternity department to find the senior night staff looking anxious.

'Problems, Janet?' Lee enquired.

'Maybe,' said the night nurse. 'Baby Carter had a convulsion this morning, about half an hour ago, and her temp's right up.'

Lee interpreted her expression. 'And you suspect meningitis?'

Janet nodded. 'Might not be. . .'

'I'll get Dr Norton to look at her,' said Lee. 'As a matter of urgency. Baby Carter? She's only three days old, isn't she?'

Janet nodded again. 'It was a prolonged labour, if you recall. Mrs C's still feeling rather weak, and suffering post-natal depression. She's not breast-feeding. This could set her back even further.'

Lee frowned. 'Indeed it could.'

When Dr Aileen Norton, the paediatrician, arrived a

short time later, Trent was with her. Lee accompanied them into the nursery, and, as the nurses there could give any assistance required, she left them. She did not expect to see Trent again, but he came to her office some time later.

When she called 'Come in!' to the knock on her door, she was not expecting him, and at the sight of his tall figure her heart flipped. Was this austere medical man really one and the same Trent Allingham who had made love to her a week ago? Who had looked so ludicrous—so sexy—in her dressing-gown?

'How's the Carter baby?' she asked on a painful swallow.

He came in and stood by the desk. 'Aileen's having blood tests done. And a lumbar puncture, of course. We won't be sure just yet whether it's bacterial, viral or aseptic. She'll need barrier nursing to avoid any spread of infection.'

'Does Mrs Carter know yet?'

'No, and I think it might be best to keep it from her until we're sure, and if it is meningitis we'll need to be somewhat circumspect in this case, I feel. She's not in good shape, and telling her that although the baby will certainly recover we can't tell what the prognosis may be won't help her.'

Lee saw his point. 'No, she'll be more anxious than ever if she thinks there's a chance the baby might have neurological problems later on, or even be deaf.' She felt deep sympathy for the young mother. Not knowing whether your child would be faced with learning difficulties or other problems could mean years of anxiety, as the deficiencies that could be caused by meningitis did not always show up immediately.

'She mustn't be kept in the dark entirely,' said Trent,

'but it might be wise to wait until she's mentally able to cope, before we explain.' He paused, frowning. 'One of the difficult situations we sometimes find ourselves in. Make sure *all* your staff know how to handle it. Especially as you won't be here for a fortnight. Aileen suggests Mrs Carter stays in for a week or so longer, and I agree.'

Lee struggled with an urge to tell him that after today she would not be there at all, that someone else would be taking his orders and doing his bidding permanently. She felt guilty again. What she was planning was not what she would approve of in anyone else, but the circumstances were mitigating. Surely she had a right to think of herself at least once in her life? She had to get away from this situation before it destroyed her. And now was her opportunity.

There was a lengthy silence, until Lee, uneasily squirming under Trent's sombre grey gaze, asked, 'Is there anything else?'

He said slowly, 'You obviously haven't changed your mind.'

'No.' The single syllable was as painful to utter as a wholc speech.

'What about Shannon?'

Lee moistened her lips nervously. 'Trent, I don't think we should discuss personal matters in the hospital. . .'

'Where else?' His voice was harsh. 'It won't take more than a few words to settle one thing. Are you going to tell Shannon who I am?'

She could not bear the intensity of his gaze. 'It might be better. . .' Her voice cracked, and she bit her lip hard to stop from crying.

'If I stopped bothering you.' There was bitterness in his voice and expression.

'Maybe. . .' she whispered, wishing he had not chosen this moment to put her through an emotional wringer.

'It would make things easier for you, wouldn't it?' he grated. 'But that's not the issue, is it? We have to decide what's best for Shannon. Just as we have to decide what's best for Mrs Carter and her baby.'

'It's not a clinical problem!' Lee flared.

'It's not a subjective decision!' he flashed back.

They glared at each other, tension high, emotion all but breaking the surface.

'What do you suggest?' Lee asked quietly. 'I think the decision has to be yours, Trent. If you want Shannon to know who you are, I haven't the right to stop you telling her.' She turned away and looked out of the window. The inlet glittered in the sunshine, but even as she looked a large cloud obscured the sun and a dark shadow engulfed the town. She felt its coldness touch her heart.

Trent eventually spoke. 'You don't give me much choice, Lee. You make me sound so utterly selfish, wanting to know my own daughter. But for Shannon's sake, perhaps, for the moment anyway, it would be best if she doesn't know. It may only unsettle her. Perhaps you're right and it would also be best if I don't see her again. Maybe, when she's older, and understands. . .'

She turned to look at him. Was his decision for Shannon's sake, or for his own? Was he covering up a subconscious relief?

'Very well,' she agreed.

The way he looked at her, she was afraid he had read

her mind, as he had sometimes seemed to. But he said nothing except, 'See you when you get back, then. Enjoy yourselves. You can say hello to Shannon for me.' There was only a trace of reproach in his voice.

When he had gone, Lee took some minutes to compose herself. The past few minutes had proved one thing: that she was wise to be leaving. How could she possibly work with Trent now? How could they ever become just friends?

CHAPTER ELEVEN

LOOKING back over the months that followed her departure from Shearwater Inlet, Lee felt she had been living in a kind of vacuum. It was almost like the time when her father had died and she had lost her grip on reality temporarily. Then, Trent had provided a bulwark to lean on, but this time she had had to cope on her own, without even Callie and family to help.

Being totally responsible for Shannon for the first time in her life had been a sobering and learning experience. Lee realised how little she had known her daughter, how little her daughter had known her. There had been some wonderful times, and some difficult ones too, but Lee felt that on balance they had come out all right. They got along as well as could be expected. Lee knew that she had a great deal to thank Callie and Nick for in the way her daughter had been brought up, and she was determined to build on it.

Settling in Melbourne had been a great adventure for Shannon, and she had enjoyed the search for a flat and a new school, finding agistment for Pastry and joining a pony club. All had been achieved without too many hassles. The hassles were all in Lee's mind, the lingering regrets and guilt feelings because of what she had done—rejecting Trent and walking out on the hospital.

Bryce had been put out when she had contacted him after the first week of the holiday to say she was resigning to work in Melbourne, and she had been on the point of telling him the whole story, but somehow on the telephone it was impossible. All she could do was cite personal reasons and apologise. She felt worse when she received a glowing reference from him.

It was some compensation to be back at the South City General hospital where she had trained, and she enjoyed nursing on the children's wards. This time she did not hide the fact that she had a daughter, but neither did she flaunt it. Those who found out usually assumed she was widowed or divorced. Shannon apparently still told anyone who was interested that her father had run off and left them when she was a baby. There was a certain romantic aura to it, even though she was not unique. 'I'm not the only one, Mum,' she told Lee. 'There are two kids in my class whose mothers are single parents.'

The principal of the school Shannon attended, when he met Lee, glanced at her bare left hand and, without batting an eyelid, called her *Ms* Dennison. Although she felt uncomfortable at the many more school functions which Shannon wanted her to attend, she braved them, and rarely encountered any real curiosity. Melbourne was different from rural communities; her private life was not as much a topic for curiosity or speculation.

It was the same at the hospital. After a while, she relaxed and began to accept that her unmarried status was only a problem to her.

She was able to organise her shifts to suit Shannon's school hours and most days picked her up after school, as well as dropping her off in the mornings. There was always someone there early. Lee's eight-till-four shift was slightly outside the normal hours, but the hospital was accommodating, and she wasn't the only one favoured.

One afternoon in November, when Shannon was staying late at school for sports practice, Lee decided to slip into the city and browse around for a new dress. There was a hospital function coming up, and Philip Rowton, a young paediatrican, had invited her along. Shannon would stay over with a friend.

Lee had not cultivated a social life and had rarely been out even to parties, but Philip had been persistent, so in the end she had said yes. He was a pleasant man, whom she got on well with, and sitting at home watching television night after night did become boring.

Luck was with her, and she found a smart little deep green dress in a silky material, with a softly flared skirt and cap sleeves, in almost the first shop she tried. It emphasised her eyes, and went well with her blonde hair. She had let the red grow out and now wore her hair longer. Lee wasn't sure why she'd changed back to her natural colour unless it was that a change of hair colour was subconsciously her way to underline a complete change in her life, as it had once before, when she had left home.

There was still plenty of time before she must pick up Shannon, so she strolled into a bookshop, hoping to find a few bargains. She was absorbed in reading a blurb on a dust cover when a voice at her elbow exclaimed,

'Lee Dennison—what a surprise!' Francine Kennedy clasped her hand, and still holding it, with a query in her eyes, said, 'Trent told me you'd left Shearwater.'

'Yes. I only went back there to look after my father,' Lee heard herself saying, 'I never intended to stay permanently.' She wished she could have run into anyone but Francine. She was surprised to see the large diamond glittering on Francine's left hand and wondered if Trent had put it there. She felt instinctively that he must have.

'I wasn't sure at first it was you,' Francine went on. 'You used to be a redhead.'

'I'm naturally blonde,' Lee explained.

Francine nodded approval. 'It suits you.' She went on, 'Trent's back in Sydney—you knew that?'

Lee didn't. She'd had no contact with the hospital since she'd left. Her only contact with Shearwater had been when she'd gone back quietly to pick up the rest of her belongings and tell Lana and Geoff what she was doing. They had jumped at the opportunity of buying the business, which had meant a swift and smooth transaction, allowing Lee to buy her own flat in Melbourne almost at once. It had been a painful wrench cutting all her ties with the place, but she believed it was for the best.

'No, I didn't know.' So she hadn't been wrong about him when she'd said he wouldn't stay long in Shearwater.

'He's just put Hilsborough on the market,' Francine told her. 'He would have done so earlier, but I managed to persuade him to wait until the refurbishing was finished so he'd get a better price.' She heaved a sigh. 'What a job! It took months longer than I anticipated. I can tell you I was glad when it was finished. The house is splendid now, but it was a lot of work. I was up and down from Sydney so often—I felt bound to supervise all the work personally, as it was for Trent.'

And you wanted every opportunity to see him, Lee thought. Why not? She glanced at Francine's ring again. They ought to be happy. They were the same kind of people. Perhaps it was just as well she had met Francine today. Knowing Trent was married to someone else might help her to forget him.

'. . .and at one stage I thought it'd never be finished before the wedding,' Francine was saying, jolting her back from her private thoughts.

'When are you getting married?' Lee managed to ask without, she hoped, betraying her feelings.

'In a fortnight.' Francine actually blushed as she added, 'It's silly really. I've been married before, but it was never like this. I'm in a real spin. Clive is just the most wonderful thing that's ever happened to me.'

Lee couldn't help her mouth dropping open. 'Clive?' she echoed.

'Trent's architect. I guess it was love at first sight.' Francine laughed. 'To be honest, I kept finding excuses to come to Melbourne on the pretence that it was to consult him about Hilsborough. Of course, that didn't last long. We soon found other things to talk about and no excuses needed!'

Lee had been so sure Francine was engaged to Trent that she could hardly take it in. She put the book she had been browsing through back on the shelf. 'I'm glad you're happy,' she said. So Trent was still a free spirit after all. She ought to have known that.

'I wish I could say the same about Trent,' Francine said, frowning anxiously. 'He's been like a bear with a sore head ever since you quit the hospital.' She eyed Lee quizzically. 'I thought you two would have hit it off perfectly.'

'I thought if he married anyone, it would be you.'

Francine laughed. 'Me? Oh, no, you were barking up the wrong tree there, Lee. Trent and me? We're chalk and cheese.'

Lee dared to say, 'But surely you were lovers?'

Now Francine looked shocked. 'No, never. Good friends, but never lovers. What made you think that?'

Lee felt embarrassed. 'Sorry. You were at Hilsborough a lot, and I just got the impression. . . I imagine he has lots of women friends.'

'You mean you saw him as a bit of a playboy?'

'Well, he isn't married,' Lee said defensively. 'And he always had lots of girlfriends when he was younger.'

Francine looked at her curiously. 'I don't think you know much about Trent Allingham now, Lee. He might behave like a perennial bachelor, but since I've got to know him better I've come to the conclusion that he's basically a frustrated family man. The trouble is he just hasn't met the right woman yet. He was so elated about Hilsborough and kept on about wanting it to be a real family home, and he was so keen for me to talk to you about the renovations, I thought you must be the reason he wanted to stay in Shearwater. And believe me, I didn't keep coming down to see Trent—it was work, and of course the chance to see Clive!'

Lee suddenly remembered Shannon. She looked at her watch. 'I'm sorry, I must go. I—I've got to pick someone up in a few minutes, and I'm already late.' She held out her hand. 'It was nice seeing you, Francine, and all the best for the wedding.'

'It was lovely seeing you,' Francine smiled. 'Shall I give your regards to Trent?'

Lee tightened her lips. 'Sure. Sorry to rush off like this. Good luck.' She hurried out of the shop and leapt on to a tram to take her to where she'd left her car. Shannon would be mad at her for being late.

Meeting Francine churned Lee up, and for several days afterwards she could hardly concentrate on her work because Trent's face kept drifting across her mind, sometines smiling, sometimes reproachful, and always tearing her heart apart. But he'd gone back to Sydney just as she'd thought he would. It vindicated her decision not to marry him. Would Francine tell him she'd seen her? she wondered.

'How would you like a spell in Obstetrics?' the DON asked her one day. 'You've had a lot of experience in that area, and we need a competent charge sister down there.'

'I'd like it,' said Lee. 'I don't really mind where I nurse, so long as I can do the same hours.'

There was no problem about that, so she moved to the obstetrics department. It was a large department, with a number of wards and private rooms, as well as nurseries, accommodation for parents and day-rooms. Lee found herself with several wards to supervise, and a constantly busy schedule.

She didn't mind. Being busy kept her thoughts in check. It was at night, lying alone in the darkness, that she could not control them.

After one such wakeful night, she arrived at the hospital feeling thoroughly jaded, and determined to put Trent right out of her mind once and for all. It was all water under the bridge, she told herself as she checked the medications out for the morning round with one of the other nurses, and made a list of supplies which were needed.

A second nurse joined them, apologetic because she had been delayed and Lee had had to do what was normally her duty. She was married and her little boy had been unwell.

'I'm sure he does it on purpose to make me stay home,' she sighed. 'He says he hates kindergarten.'

Lee sympathised. 'They go through stages, Ellen. Don't worry—you're not all that late, and we're fairly quiet this morning. But if you two can manage, I've got a few piles of paperwork to vanquish.' As the two nurses went out with the medications trolley, Lee signed the book and locked the cupboard.

She hurried back to her office, a slight figure in blue jacket and white dress, her blonde hair clipped neatly back behind her ears. She heard the big swing doors behind her squeak open and reminded herself to ask Maintenance to oil them. Hearing male voices, she glanced perfunctorily over her shoulder to see who had come through—it was a little early for doctors' rounds. There were two men, one in a white coat, the other in a pale grey suit. Lee saw only the man in the suit, the tall, broad figure with penetrating grey eyes and dark waving hair. He was talking earnestly to his companion, the senior registrar, and had not yet noticed her.

'Trent. . .' she breathed in dismay, and scuttled quickly into her office.

CHAPTER TWELVE

IMAGINATION, Lee told herself, leaning against the closed door. Hallucination. Just somebody who looks like him. Plenty of tall, dark and handsome doctors around, even ones with eyes that can persuade you they can see into your soul. The trouble is, my girl, you didn't get enough sleep last night. Somehow you've got to stop thinking about him. . .

She crossed to her desk, sat down and stared at the pile of paperwork before her. Patients' names swam in a mist. Lee wiped her hand across her eyes, then got up again and poured herself a glass of water from the jug on the windowsill. She stared vacantly out of the window at the cityscape, with its glass-walled skyscrapers glinting hypnotically in the sun. *Imagination*. . .

'Oh, God, I love him so much,' she whispered, hugging herself. Tears ran down her face until the telephone's shrill summons froze her emotions, forcing her to flick the tears away and answer it. 'Sister Dennison.'

'A and E. A Mrs Woodrow has just arrived. We're sending her up. The baby's on the way, a week early, according to her.'

'All right. Thanks.'

It wasn't unusual. Babies mostly seemed to arrive early or late. Lee switched off her personal pain and geared herself to admit the patient and prepare for the imminent birth. For one awful moment she hesitated at the door, half afraid to go out into the corridor in case he was there, half desperately wanting him to be. But he can't be, she reminded herself. It was just imagination.

Mrs Woodrow was made comfortable, her contractions timed and the usual tests on blood and urine done. She was having her fourth child and was quite relaxed about it all.

'Never had a moment's trouble,' she said, and laughing, 'I must be made for babies. The only thing is they always come early. I told my doctor, but he reckoned it would be next week.' She looked smug. 'Doctors don't know everything.'

'No, they can't know everything,' Lee agreed absently, rolling up the sphygmomanometer cuff after noting the patient's blood pressure reading on the chart. 'You seem to be in pretty good shape, Mrs Woodrow.'

'Shannon,' said the mother-to-be in a friendly tone. She patted the mound below her breasts. 'Might call this one Shannon after me if it's a girl. Tom's got his Thomas junior and we named the other two for grandparents, so I reckon it's my turn. What do you think of Shannon as a name, Sister?'

'I think it's a pretty name,' said Lee. 'My daughter's name is Shannon.'

The patient opened her mouth to answer, but was racked by a contraction. When she could speak again, she said with a grin, 'This is when I always say "never again"!'

Lee wiped the perspiration from her face. 'Won't be long now.'

Another nurse came in, a junior, and Lee said, 'I'll see you later, Shannon. Sally will be on hand if you want anything.' To the nurse she said in a low tone, 'Don't leave her alone for long. This is when they need the most encouragement, even the experienced ones. If they think you've forgotten them, they panic.'

Sally nodded and looked confident. Lee briefly thought of how she had been when younger even than this girl, having a baby herself, panic-stricken, guilt-ridden, and all alone, feeling that her whole world had come crumbling down about her. It seemed like half a lifetime away, yet it also felt like only yesterday.

Shannon Woodrow was delivered of a baby girl half an hour before Lee's shift was over. She did not assist at the actual birth, but she slipped in to see the new mother soon afterwards. The baby was already eagerly discovering that survival meant knowing where sustenance came from.

'She's beautiful,' smiled Lee, thinking of her own Shannon and how from the moment she had seen the tiny, wizened, red-faced little scrap of life, she had known, with all the fierce maternal instinct of a tigress, that her decision to keep her baby was right.

'She was worth it,' said Shannon Woodrow with a drowsy smile. 'Tom's going to be mad that he missed the fun. They eventually got him on his car phone, and he's on the way. Pity he couldn't have been here, but he saw the other three born. Nice, I think, for the father to be present, don't you, Sister?'

'Yes—yes, of course. It's a wonderful experience,' Lee agreed.

She walked slowly back to her office wrapped in her own thoughts, which the birth of her daughter's namesake had winged back to that traumatic time more than eleven years ago. How wonderful it would have been if Trent had been there to hold her hand, wipe her brow and murmur encouragement.

When she opened the door she did not see him at

first. She marched in quickly and closed the door behind her, anxious to finish the task she had been doing and go to meet Shannon. Maybe they'd go to a film and have a Chinese take-away afterwards, she thought. Shannon liked that sort of treat. . . Her thoughts stopped dead, as did her feet. Trent was standing by the window looking at the view. He turned round.

'Hello, Lee.'

Was there still blood in her veins? To Lee it didn't seem like it. 'Hello, Trent,' she said, dry-mouthed.

He looked her over, coolly, clinically, but with approval. 'You've changed your hair,' he said. 'It's blonde and longer. . . I didn't recognise you at first, out in the corridor a while ago.'

Lee got a grip on herself. 'What are you doing at the SCG?' she asked.

'I came down for a conference on obstetrics.'

'Another one? Must be great always going to conferences. Trips interstate.' Why was she making her remarks sound like innuendo?

Trent gave no sign of noticing. 'I met an old colleague, your consultant obstetrician, John Stockdale. He invited me to take a look around. Things have changed quite a bit since I was last here.'

Again she forestalled the silence by hurrying on, 'I met Francine one day in the city. She said you'd left Shearwater and were selling Hilsborough.'

'Yes, she mentioned she'd seen you.'

'Did the wedding go off all right?'

'Without a hitch. It was very nice. Rather formal, but *nice*.' He sounded mocking. 'Very North Shore. Very Francine!'

'She looked beautiful, I'm sure. She seemed very happy,' Lee said.

'I hope so.' He paused, then added, 'I gave her away.'

Lee's face showed a flicker of surprise. 'Oh? Really?'

'Her father's dead and I'm her best friend, so she says. Especially as I introduced her to Clive. We've known each other for years.'

He moved quickly to stand close to her, sliding his hand around her neck and into her hair. 'I always liked your hair blonde and long. It's not long enough yet. . . but getting there. . .' His eyes darkened with involuntary desire, and Lee felt the charge between them as strongly as ever.

'No. . .' she whispered.

Trent touched his lips to hers. 'Francine couldn't remember which hospital you'd told her you were working at. I rather hoped it might be here.'

Lee wrenched herself away. 'Trent, this is ridiculous. Will you please go?'

He had no intention of going yet. God, she looked beautiful. They said absence made the heart grow fonder. It did more than that. It had made love, desire, anxiety and the whole gamut of other emotions threaten to overwhelm him. He wanted to hold, touch, possess. . . But he mustn't blow it this time. This was his last chance. He got a grip on himself, spoke evenly, naturally. 'How's Shannon?'

She felt numb. Numbed with shock, and a weird kind of happiness. She had as much trouble controlling herself as Trent. 'She's fine. She likes her school and, according to her, living in Melbourne is *rad*.'

He chuckled. 'Because she can go and watch the Daimaru clock strike as often as she likes?' There was laughter in the grey eyes now, and an insidious reminder of the intimacy of that day they'd met him at Melbourne Central.

Lee suppressed the pang it gave her. 'I'm afraid the novelty of that soon wore off.' She began tidying her desk. 'I'm off duty in a few minutes. I've a few things to do before I hand over, so if you'll excuse me. . .'

'We could have dinner.' His options were few.

She faced him. 'I'm taking Shannon to a film and we'll have a take-away afterwards.'

He risked a second rebuff. 'You could invite me along. I'd like to see Shannon, just this once,' he said.

Lee couldn't cope with it, it was too sudden. 'No. You agreed, remember, it's better that you don't.'

'You've told her about me?'

'No.'

'If she still thinks I'm just a friend, what harm can it do?'

It can do a lot of harm to me, Lee thought, but remained silent.

Trent gripped her shoulders, his resolve disintegrating. 'I still want to marry you, Lee. It wasn't just a passing phase. That's what you thought, wasn't it? So for God's sake, what do I have to do to make you understand?'

She caught her top lip between her teeth and bit hard. 'It's still only because of Shannon you want to marry me, not *me*.'

'Lee, I wanted you before I knew about Shannon.'

'In your bed. Not for keeps, though. Trent, you got sick of Shearwater and went back to Sydney, as I said you would. You'd hate being tied down by marriage. And when Shannon's grown up and living her own life, what then?'

He raked both hands through his hair, and faced her

angrily. 'Damn and blast you, Lee! You and your stubborn logic and pride. Why do I humiliate myself like this?'

'Please go, Trent,' she said. 'I'm still on duty and I have a lot to do.'

He gave her a long hard look, then did as she asked. The door closed slowly behind him, and Lee bit her lip even harder to stem the tears that threatened.

A few minutes later she walked across the car park to her secondhand hatchback and tried to shift her thoughts on to the prospect of a new car. It was time she got something that she didn't have to spend half her life repairing. She could afford it now. She slid into the driver's seat and put the key in the ignition.

Five minutes later she was peering into the engine and cursing the car for choosing this moment to play up and refuse to start. For once she couldn't even diagnose what was wrong.

'What's up?'

Lee lifted her head out of the engine to look into Trent's questioning gaze. Anger flared. Why couldn't he leave her alone?

'My car won't start,' she said through clenched teeth as she slammed the bonnet down. 'Excuse me, I'll have to call the RACV and phone Shannon's school to tell them I'll be late.'

'It would save time if I drove you, and you could call the RACV from home,' he suggested.

She mouthed a refusal, but he got in first. He caught hold of her arm. 'Come on, Lee, at least let me do you a favour.'

She was late already. She made a quick decision. 'All right. Thanks.' She sounded ungracious, but couldn't help it.

Shannon was playing netball when Lee arrived at the school. She was used to her mother not always being prompt, understood why and did not complain.

'Where's the car?' she asked, looking around as they came out of the school gates.

'It broke down,' Lee told her, grimacing. 'Again! We really will have to get a new one.'

'So how did you get here? Taxi?' Shannon asked, looking for it.

'No, a friend gave me a lift. Someone you know.' Lee pointed across the road to where Trent was standing by the hire car waiting for them, and saw Shannon's face light up when she recognised him.

'Trent!' she yelled. She bounded across the road towards him. In a split second of horror, Lee heard Trent shout, 'Look out!' as a car swung round the corner fast. Brakes screeched, but it still caught Shannon a glancing blow and tossed her like a rag doll into the air. Her schoolbag arced almost to Lee's feet. For another second Lee stood in frozen disbelief, then she ran to the still, crumpled figure that lay face down on the roadway.

'Shannon!' she heard herself screaming over and over.

'Don't move her!' It was Trent, so calm it was unreal, but with a ring of authority that checked even Lee. 'She might have spinal injuries.'

The driver stood pale and shaking beside them, saying, 'She just ran out. I didn't see her.'

Trent said urgently to the small crowd that had run to the scene at the sound of squealing brakes. 'Somebody ring an ambulance. Quickly!'

Lee looked at him fearfully. 'Is she—dead?'

He was bending over the pale face of their daughter,

his fingers probing for the carotid artery. He turned quickly to Lee. 'She's not breathing and there's no pulse. We need to do CPR. Are you up to it?'

Not breathing. No pulse. Shannon was dead. Lee felt the pain, but knew she must not accept it without a fight. Shannon could be brought back to life.

'We'll have to turn her over,' Trent said. 'Very gently—you know how.' First he checked that the airway was clear, and gently probed with his fingers to make sure there was no mucus or obstructions in the child's mouth, then he and Lee shifted her gingerly on to her back, Lee praying that they would not do any further damage. Trent said briskly, 'You do the respirations, I'll do the compressions. One inflation to five compressions. OK? Start now!'

Lee concentrated her mind. She forced herself not to think of the limp figure on the roadway as her daughter but as a patient who had suffered a cardiac arrest, who needed urgent attention, attention she could give, had given many times.

She tilted Shannon's chin and breathed air into her lungs, sealing her nose with her cheek. She glanced at Trent, counted the compressions, breathed again. For three and a half minutes they worked in perfect unison, twelve cycles a minute, and then thankfully Lee heard the ambulance siren. Hurry! she urged silently. There was still a chance. Four minutes, they said, before irreversible brain damage occurred, but some said less, and sometimes people were revived after a longer time with no impairment. Lee checked the carotid. Was there a pulse? She was trembling too much to be sure.

'One, two. . .' Trent was counting, and Lee bent her head to the rhythm once more. For a moment she thought she was dreaming when she heard a convulsive cough and saw Shannon's eyelids flicker briefly, her body twitch of its own accord.

'Trent. . .'

'We've got her,' he said quietly, as the ambulance crew piled out of their vehicle and converged on them, taking over the resuscitation with their high-technology equipment.

Lee watched helplessly as an oxygen mask covered Shannon's face, and one of the paramedics slid a hypodermic into her arm. Were they giving her the right drug, the right dose? Did they know what they were doing? Why didn't they get a move on? She saw a stain on her dress. Blood. Shannon's blood. Oh, God, she might be bleeding to death and they didn't know. The actions of Trent and the ambulance crew seemed to be happening in unbearable slow motion. Lee jerked forward, and was held back by strong hands.

'Take it easy,' Trent said, and held her against him. 'You can go with her if you like.'

Lee realised that for a moment her control had almost deserted her. She mumbled, 'Sorry,' and let him help her into the ambulance. One of the paramedics handed her the drip, saying, 'You're a nurse, I gather. Keep an eye on this, would you? We've got some first aid to see to.'

Something to do to help was what Lee needed. All the way to the hospital, she held the drip with one hand, and Shannon's hand with the other, and prayed, while the ambulance men staunched a profusely bleeding wound on Shannon's leg. She had breathed life back into her precious daughter, and Trent had massaged her heart into restarting, but was it enough? What other injuries did Shannon have? She knew Trent was afraid of spinal injury which the necessary force of

CPR could have aggravated. Anyone hit and thrown as Shannon had been was not going to get off with a flesh wound in her leg. She had looked like a rag doll flying through the air—an image that would stay with Lee for a long time—but unlike a doll, she had bones and ligaments and tendons, and fragile organs. Lee watched the drip and the oxygen anxiously, frantic in case they suddenly stopped functioning properly during the interminable trip to the hospital.

That Trent had followed closely behind in his car she was aware as soon as they arrived. She was again standing helplessly by as orderlies hurried Shannon away from her when a hand rested on her shoulder and she felt the pressure of reassuring fingers. She looked up into Trent's tense face.

'Come on,' he said, 'let's go in.'

It was strange walking into her own hospital casualty department as the relative of a victim. Lee did not know the nurse who took details.

'You're her mother?'

'Yes.'

The nurse glanced at Trent. 'Father?'

He said firmly, 'Yes,' and Lee looked at him, her lips parted to speak, but she said nothing. She answered the rest of the questions, then Trent said, 'Lee's a nurse here, Sister, and I'm a visiting doctor. All right if we go through?'

The nurse looked startled but did not try to stop them. 'They've taken her straight to Theatre,' she said. 'You won't be able to see her yet.'

'We know. We'll find somewhere to wait.'

There was a small ante-room near the OR suite where Trent installed Lee while he went to find out what he could. Lee waited in nail-biting suspense for him to come back. When he did, he brought her a cup of coffee and one for himself.

'Did you find out anything?' Lee asked anxiously.

He shook his head. 'Nothing definite.' He clasped her hand in his. 'It might not be as bad as you think.'

Her anguish welled up and she rested her head against his shoulder. 'If she dies. . .'

Trent held her close, stroking her back soothingly. 'She mustn't die. We won't let her die, Lee. Will we?' He tilted her face and looked steadily into her brimming eyes. 'Will we?'

Lee rolled her lips tightly together, over and over, trying to stem the tears. 'No,' she whispered, and clenched her fists in her lap.

After a few minutes, Trent got up. 'I'll go and see if there's any news yet.' He squeezed her hand tightly. 'Won't be long.'

He was gone for only five minutes. When he came back his face was grave. He sat down beside her again, holding both her hands in his. She looked at him with mute appeal, afraid to ask.

'It's going to be a long haul,' he said. 'She has multiple injuries—fractured pelvis, ruptured spleen, compound arm and leg fractures, but she won't be quadra- or paraplegic.'

'Thank God for that!' But there was still something vital he had not mentioned. Fearfully, Lee asked, 'Head injuries. . .?'

Trent gripped her hands hard. 'They don't know yet. She's unconscious, but she may not be in a coma.'

She wrested her hands from his and covered her face. 'Oh, my poor darling. Oh, Shannon. . .' She looked at Trent. 'I've never felt so *helpless*.'

He was shaking his head. 'Nor me.' His features

contorted in anguish and he bent his head, clasping his hands behind his neck and resting his elbows on his knees, staring at the floor.

'It was my fault,' he grated in a low voice. 'If I hadn't been there, she wouldn't have dashed across the road. . .' His shoulders shook convulsively as emotion found its outlet. 'If I hadn't insisted on coming with you . . .on seeing her. . .'

Lee stared at him for a moment, nonplussed. Blaming him had never occurred to her. Suddenly she was the comforter. She put her arms around him.

'Trent, it wasn't your fault. It wasn't anybody's fault. Only Shannon's perhaps for running without looking. . .'

'Because she saw me on the other side of the road. . .'

'She was excited. Trent, it wasn't your fault.'

He leaned back, hands still clasped behind his head, eyes closed. 'It was my fault a long time ago,' he said slowly. 'If I hadn't made love to you. . .'

Lee took a deep breath. 'Trent, I don't blame you for that.'

'Don't you?' His words were bitter, his eyes bleak. 'Of course you do. If I'd acted more responsibly you wouldn't have had your life ruined.'

Lee said quietly, 'It wasn't ruined. I didn't have to have Shannon, Trent. I chose to. I wanted her.'

'Why?'

She said very softly, 'You must know why. Because I loved you, of course.'

He drew her into his arms, resting his head against her breast, and Lee stroked his hair gently. They were interrupted by a nurse in theatre gear entering, and drew apart quickly. It was the theatre runner. She came in hesitantly.

'Dr Morley asked me to tell you that the operations on your daughter will take some time. He said it would be best if you went home.' She looked sympathetically at each in turn. 'It's won't be possible for you to see Shannon for several hours. We'll call you as soon as she's transferred to an ICU. Make sure Sister has your phone number.'

When she had gone, Trent looked questioningly at Lee. 'We aren't doing much good sitting here, are we?'

'I want to be near her,' said Lee. 'In case. . .'

'They'll let us know,' Trent insisted. 'I think perhaps we ought to go, Lee. We could go and have a meal and come back.'

'I couldn't eat. . .'

He stood up and held out his hand. 'Come on, let's go. You'll be able to relax better at home. I'll drive you.'

Lee felt dazed. Uncertainly, she stood up, and almost collapsed in his arms. Trent held her firmly. 'I forgot about my car,' she said. 'I should have rung the RACV.'

'We'll do that,' he promised.

Although Lee hated leaving the hospital while Shannon was so critical, there was a sense of relief at walking into the familiar surroundings of her flat, and she slumped thankfully on to the couch. It was less than ten minutes' drive to the hospital. They could be there very quickly if summoned.

Trent asked if she had any brandy, and poured them both one. He did not join her on the couch, but sat in an armchair. It was comforting having him there.

The brandy steadied her, and gradually her strength

and resilience reasserted itself. 'I'll make something to eat,' she said at last.

Trent followed her into the kitchen and made tea while she toasted sandwiches. They didn't talk much then or later. Lee switched on the television, but neither she nor Trent could concentrate on the programme. It was just there to fill the silence.

When the telephone rang, Lee got up and ran to it, her heart beating frantically. Trent was behind her, his hands tightly encircling her waist even as she said, 'Hello.'

A few seconds later she replaced the receiver. 'She's out of Theatre,' she said in a tense little voice. 'We can go and see her in Intensive Care.'

Trent's answer was to squeeze her tightly, give her a reassuring smile, and drop a light kiss on her mouth. Then he said, 'She'll make it, Lee. I know she will.'

To Lee, the intensive care unit with which she was ordinarily so familiar had suddenly become a fearsome place, with its electronic wizardry. The drips which hung above the inert form in the stark white bed were suddenly a threat, the tubes in her daughter's body a violation, the flickering monitors a reminder that keeping a body alive was not always enough. She knew now how relatives of patients felt when they first saw a loved one so enmeshed in technology, why their faith in medical skills was sometimes shaken, their fears overwhelming.

But Lee was a nurse, an experienced sister, and her gut reactions were fleeting. Her practised eye ran quickly over the life-saving equipment that cluttered the room and crowded around the bed. She knew how it worked, what it was doing, and her trained mind could interpret the language of technology.

Both she and Trent had been gowned and masked. Their eyes met across Shannon's bed, and it was an exchange of confidence. Lee felt Trent's strength reach out to her and knew she must return it. He needed support as much as she did. Shannon was as much his flesh and blood as she was hers.

There was nothing they could do but look. Lee looked long and steadily at the pale face with its tubes and bandages and with every fibre of her being willed the child to pull through. She knew Trent was doing the same.

Their eyes met again and Lee said with bitter humour, 'She'll hate having her head shaved.'

She heard him give a choked kind of reply. He grasped her hand as they went out, and all that he was feeling was conveyed through the pressure of his fingers.

Lee couldn't let him go back to his hotel. He drove her home and he stayed the night. Because they still needed to share the crisis, they shared her bed, lying side by side but at first not touching. There was too much other shared emotion for desire, and when they finally slept in each other's arms it was for another kind of need. Lee's sleep was light because her subconscious was alert for the telephone, as no doubt Trent's was too. That it did not ring was a signal of hope.

They went together to the hospital next morning. Lee felt calmer now the first shock was fading, but her limbs were still weak and she was glad of Trent's arm to slip hers through as they made their way to the intensive care unit where Shannon lay.

The surgeon, whom Lee knew slightly, was just coming out. He drew them aside. Lee took comfort from the fact that he was smiling.

'How is she?' she asked.

'Responding well,' he answered. 'She has serious injuries, as you'd expect in that kind of accident, but her youth and natural resilience will help to pull her through.'

He was matter-of-fact, unemotional, totally professional, and that meant more to Lee than anything. He wasn't trying to fool her. She trusted him.

Shannon was still heavily sedated, but conscious. She recognised them both and managed a faint smile. Her lips moved almost imperceptibly, but Lee caught the whispered, 'Sorry, Mummy,' which nearly made her break down. Shannon looked at Trent, smiled faintly and said, 'Hi!'

They were permitted to stay only for a few minutes now, and perhaps a short time later in the day. Tomorrow, they were told, it would be longer.

Trent insisted on taking Lee to lunch. They tried to talk about everything except Shannon, but she kept creeping back into the conversation. Trent had spoken for a few minutes to the surgeon, while Lee was talking to the sister in charge of the ICU, and Lee kept thinking of questions she wanted answered.

She decided she would go back to work the next day. 'I'll be on the spot if anything happens,' she said. 'I can go and see her more often.'

Trent agreed. 'And working will help to keep your mind off things.'

'When are you going back?' Lee asked, not looking at him, not wanting to betray that she didn't want him to go, that she needed him there, at least for a while.

Trent was decisive. 'Not till Shannon's out of the wood.'

'What about your job in Sydney?'

'They can manage without me.'

'I appreciate it,' Lee said slowly. 'You've been a tremendous help, Trent, like you were before, when Dad died. I'm truly grateful. I—I needed someone. . .'

They were sitting in a secluded corner of a garden restaurant, with the sun shining and a fountain tinkling nearby. They'd had a late lunch and nearly all the other diners had gone, but no one was hassling them.

Trent reached for her hand. 'We all need someone, some time or other. Lee—I need you, you need me, and Shannon needs us both.'

'I know. . .' she hesitated, biting her lip. 'But I can't help being afraid. . .'

His fingers tightened around hers. 'Sometimes, Lee, we have to take chances. That's what life's all about. Even what you think is the safe ground can be risky.'

'Whatever I did, Shannon wasn't safe,' she said slowly.

'No one is totally safe. No one is totally immune from hurt and disappointment, and no one is infallible. You know I'm not. I'm human, I make mistakes. I try not to make the same ones again. But I love you—please believe that.'

Lee chewed on the words she wanted to say for a moment, then said slowly, 'I want to trust you, Trent. I think I do now. This last twenty-four hours have made me look at myself and my life all over again, to recognise the fragility of happiness, of life itself, and to see you as a person, not as what you always represented.'

'You've forgiven me for being an Allingham?'

She mustered a smile. 'I think I've come to terms with it.'

Trent listened to her with a growing hope, hardly daring to believe that his interpretation of what she was saying was the one she intended.

Lee stared into the fountain for a moment, then turned her gaze back to him. 'I wish you weren't selling Hilsborough,' she told him.

'Would you want to live there? Wouldn't the memories. . .?'

She shook her head. 'I've finally vanquished that ghost. It was pride, I suppose. And my humiliation was nothing to do with you.'

'It's not sold yet,' he said, half afraid to feel elated. 'I can take it off the market. After all, it was done up for you.'

She was startled. 'For me?'

'Yes. I was mad, I know, but I told Francine to get your ideas. I wanted Hilsborough to be your house. I wanted you there, with me.'

Lee smiled. 'But, Trent, you're working back in Sydney. . .and it's a bit large for a holiday home.'

'I can go back to Shearwater any time,' he said. 'I'd be happy to. My roots are there, but I found it intolerable to be there without you. Shall we go back?'

'People will talk.'

'Of course. People like happy endings!'

Lee laughed softly. 'Yes. And Shannon will love Hilsborough.' She went on, 'I suppose Shearwater might be a bit dull for her, but she'll get used to it.'

'A couple of brothers and sisters might make a difference,' said Trent. 'The house is a bit large for just the three of us to rattle around in.' He stopped, hoping his runaway enthusiasm hadn't offended her. He was still afraid of unwittingly snapping the tenuous thread that joined them.

She nodded. 'Maybe we should ask Shannon.'

Trent leaned across the table and kissed her. 'We'd better ask her first if she minds if we get married.'

Lee unintentionally kept him in an agony of suspense before she said confidently, 'I think we both know she'll thoroughly approve.' She kissed him lightly. Then, aware of the step she had taken, she drew back a little, observing him carefully, searching her mind for the doubts that had always surfaced before whenever she had thought about marrying him, but now, miraculously, there were none.

'I love you, Lee,' he said again. 'You do believe that now, don't you?'

'Yes, I do.'

'You said you loved me all those years ago. Do you love me now?' he asked softly.

Lee did not hesitate. 'With all my heart.'

'I think,' he whispered, 'that in the end that's all that matters.'

For long moments they sat gazing into each other's eyes, smiling foolishly, then Trent said, 'I wonder if they've got any chilled champagne left?'

Lee, feeling as though champagne was already bubbling through her veins, said, 'Let's ask them.'

Trent went to find a waiter, and soon there was an ice-bucket and a bottle of vintage champagne on the table. Nobody worried that it was way past the lunch-hour and that the restaurant was now closed. Lovers must be indulged and left alone.

'Trent,' said Lee after the second glass of champagne, 'I must ask you something.'

'What's that?' He stroked her fingers lovingly.

'That day my motorbike ran out of gas. Did you milk the tank on purpose?'

To her intense gratification, his face reddened. 'I'm afraid so. I guess one of my faults is that I tend to be impulsive. I wanted to get you up to Hilsborough, alone, because seeing you again, even with that ridiculous red hair, had bowled me over completely. I was desperate to know whether seeing me again had had the same effect on you.'

Lee pouted. 'I thought red hair rather suited my personality.'

He laughed. 'True. You can be a fiery little person when you want. But the girl who had bewitched me was blonde, and I wasn't sure you were still the same person.' He reached out to her and slid his fingers along her jaw and around her nape, lifting the now blonde hair with his fingers. 'I'm glad you went back to being blonde.'

'And I'm glad you came back to Hilsborough and your car developed fan-belt trouble,' said Lee, feeling happiness spreading through her like ripples on water. 'And I'm glad to know I wasn't forgetful about the Yamaha's tank. I was worried there for a while!' She giggled involuntarily and clamped her hand over her mouth.

Trent upended the champagne bottle. It was empty. He glanced at his watch. 'We've been here for hours!'

Lee said, 'Do you think they'd let us see Shannon again now? Maybe if we tell her we're going to be married, it'll speed her recovery.'

'I hope so,' Trent said with feeling. 'I don't want to have to wait too long for a wedding.'

'Nor me.'

As Lee stood up, he gathered her firmly into his arms and kissed her, long and possessively, much to the delight and amusement of the restaurant staff, who had delayed their departure to make sure that the love story unfolding in the corner by the fountain had a happy ending.